Theodore L. Cuyler

Wayside Springs from the Fountain of Life

Theodore L. Cuyler

Wayside Springs from the Fountain of Life

ISBN/EAN: 9783337371111

Printed in Europe, USA, Canada, Australia, Japan

Cover: Foto ©Andreas Hilbeck / pixelio.de

More available books at **www.hansebooks.com**

Wayside Springs

FROM THE

FOUNTAIN OF LIFE.

BY

THEODORE L. CUYLER, D.D.,

PASTOR OF LAFAYETTE AVENUE CHURCH, BROOKLYN.

AMERICAN TRACT SOCIETY,

150 NASSAU STREET, NEW YORK.

CONTENTS

4 CONTENTS.

WAYSIDE SPRINGS.

THE SONG AT THE WELL.

THERE was once a sermon at a well. The teacher was Jesus of Nazareth, and the discourse was delivered to one poor sinful woman as the entire audience. The Son of God felt (what we ministers too often forget on stormy Sundays) that a single immortal soul is a great audience.

Other wells in the Bible are historic besides the well of Sychar. One, at Bethlehem, is associated with a princely act of chivalry; another, at Nahor, with the beginning of a singular courtship. We venture to say that there is one well beside which most of our readers never halted and out of which they have never drawn either a song or a sermon.

It was situated on the borders of Moab, not far from Mount Pisgah, whose site has lately been identified by our Palestine Exploration Society. It bears the name of Beer, which signifies a well-spring. Up to this spot thirsty Israel came on their journey from Egypt to Canaan. The Lord had just said unto Moses, "Gather the people together, and I will give them water." Here is a promise; but, like most of God's promises, it is coupled with a condition. The condition in this case is that the leaders of the congregation were to dig for the water.

A striking scene unfolds itself. The leaders of the host begin to open the loose sand with the staves which they carried. Moses directs the work, and the earth is thrown out fast. While the digging goes forward the people sing a simple song—one of the oldest snatches of song that has come down to us:

"Spring up, O well! Sing ye unto him! The princes dug it; the nobles of the people opened it, with the lawgiver's sceptre, with the staves."

Presently the cool water begins to steal in and fill up the cavity. The water bubbles up to music. The plash of the cool liquid mingles with the song of the multitude as they press forward and draw the sweet refreshment for their thirsty tongues. It is an inviting scene and is brimming with spiritual instruction. Many a sweet lesson may we draw from this outgushing well at Beer.

We learn afresh the good old truth that the Lord will provide. It is a grievous sin to doubt God or to limit the Holy One of Israel. He can open rivers in the midst of the desert, and can make the dry land to become springs of water. As long as we remain unbelieving our souls parch up with the dryness. Poor stingy, faithless professors find their religious life little better than a dull march over a very barren Sahara of formalities. There is no joy in their souls and no song on their tongues. As long as Christians neglect duty, and forswear prayer, and disobey God they must expect nothing else than drought and barrenness.

God puts his well-springs of blessing inside
the gateway of *faith*, and our faith is to be proved
by our obedience. As soon as Israel believed
God enough to dig, and as soon as the staves
were thrust into the sand, the waters began to
bubble up. The people began to work, and God
began to work also. They began to pray also;
their prayer took the form of a song. They sang
their prayer: "Spring up, O well!" Really the
deepest, richest, and devoutest hymns we sing
are full of aspiration and petition. They are
yearnings towards God and outcries for blessings.
That matchless hymn, "Jesus, lover of my soul,"
is the soul's passionate call upon Jesus to open
his bosom of love and let us hide ourselves there.
"Nearer, my God, to thee" is a prayer which
has floated up on the wings of song from thousands of yearning hearts. "Guide me, O thou
great Jehovah!" is another. When a long-thirst-
ing church is beginning to arouse into a revival, its hymns begin to become fervent soul-cries
for the power from on high. Such song is irre-
pressible. The soul bursts into it. Petition min-

gles with praise, and the heart's deepest wants are blended with the heart's fullest gratitude. While we are digging for the water and praying for the water, we are singing for thankfulness that the water begins to flow. This complex idea runs through all of David's richest Psalms. They are blended prayer and praise.

This triple process belongs to every Christian's best labors and sweetest joys. He yearns after Jesus, and after a fuller tasting of Jesus' love, and after a fuller enduement with the Spirit. With his hands he is digging, but with his lips he is singing. Duty is no longer drudgery; it is delight. Witness, all ye beloved brethren who have experienced the richest joys of revival seasons, has not preaching the Word, and praying for the conversion of sinners, and honest work for the Master been a spiritual luxury? As you plied the staves and the waters of salvation gushed out, you have taken out Israel's strain, "Spring up, O well. Sing ye unto him."

That gathering at the fountain of Beer was

2

a primitive praise-meeting. We should have many such in our churches, and if we were filled with the Spirit we would multiply our "sacrifices of praise." The more the blessings the more the joys, and the more the joys the more the music. While Israel continued to murmur against God they were parched with drought. When they began to work and to pray and to sing, the fountain burst forth. An ounce of song is worth a ton of scolding. As a group of sailors on the deck, when they pull with a will, always pull to the cadence of a song, so God's people will always pull with more harmony and strength when they join in the voice of praise. "Whoso offereth praise glorifieth Me." God never loves to hear us murmur or scold or revile each other. He loveth the prayer of faith and the upspringing of joyful praise. It was not only Paul's prayer, but Paul's midnight song of praise, that shook open the old dungeon at Philippi.

One other thought must not be forgotten as we stand by that well of Beer. Those inflowing waters are a beautiful type of the Holy Spirit.

As the previous scene of the uplifted brazen ser-
pent is a type of the atoning Saviour, so the
fountain of Beer is a symbol of the influences of
the Spirit. Christ himself employed the same
emblem, as we read in the seventh chapter of
John's Gospel. When the divine Spirit flows
into our souls, then come refreshment, peace,
strength, holiness, and the sweetest, purest of all
joys. Then we work for Christ with elastic hope.
Then we see the fruits of our toil springing up
like Beer's bursting well. Then we have the
new song put into our mouths, and our hearts
make melody. Life becomes an antepast of
heaven. We are becoming attuned for those
hallelujahs which we shall sing with rapturous
sweetness beside that crystal stream which flow-
eth out of the throne of God and of the Lamb.

CHRIST THE FOUNTAIN.

"IF any man thirst, let him come to Me and drink !" This was an astonishing announcement. If Plato had uttered it from his Academy, it would have savored of boastful presumption. Yet a Galilean peasant, whose whole "school" of followers scarcely went beyond a dozen fishermen and publicans, makes this proclamation to all human kind : "If any one is thirsty for pure happiness, I will satisfy him ; if any one is suffering from a sense of guilt, I will relieve him ; if any one is heart-broken, I will comfort him." There is no alternative. Either this carpenter's son from Galilee is an insane impostor, or else he is a being clothed with divine power. No madman ever talked for three years without uttering one foolish syllable ; no impostor ever pushed himself before the public eye for three years without doing one selfish act.

Jesus of Nazareth, then, was what he claimed to be—the Son of God.

He does not draw from others his supplies for human needs ; he invites everybody to come and draw from him. He is not a reservoir filled up from some other sources and liable to be exhausted ; he is an original, self-supplied FOUNTAIN-HEAD. Never had the face of humanity been more parched and dusty and barren than was that Oriental world when Jesus burst up through it like an artesian well. Even Judaism had become like a desert, and lo ! there breaks forth this gushing fountain of crystal waters. He is more than a teacher, giving instruction on all profound and practical questions. He is more than a miracle-worker, giving sight to the blind, ears to the deaf, and healing to the diseased. His supreme gift to man is *himself*. From himself flows forth the recovering influence ; from the inexhaustible depths of his own being, as "very God of very God," a whole thirsty race may draw refreshment. "The water that I give shall be *in you* a well of water springing up into

everlasting life.'' It is not simply profound
truths that Jesus offers, or a system of doctrine,
or a beautiful model of right living. He offers
himself as the satisfier : Drink me, take me into
your souls, and ye will never die of thirst.

What a thirsty crowd fills all the thorough-
fares of life ! Quacks cry their nostrums on every hand. Ambition sets up its dizzy ladder and
proclaims: If any man thirst for happiness, let
him come hither and climb. Mammon puts up
over the doors to his temples of traffic : If any
man thirst, let him come to me and get rich.
Pleasure lights her saloons and strings her viols
and sets out her flagons and cries aloud to the
passers-by: If any are wretched and thirst for
enjoyment, let them turn in hither and drink.
And all these are but miserable, broken cisterns,
that hold no water. In every human soul is a
crying want, a hunger that such husks cannot
feed, a thirst that grows the keener the longer it
is trifled with. My soul recognizes sin and thirsts
for relief from it. I am so weak that I have been
overthrown again and again; I want strength

equal to the conflict. My earthly sources of happiness are precarious. Death has already shattered more than one beautiful pitcher at my domestic fountain. God has put within me desires and demands that no uncertain rivulet can satisfy. My soul thirsts for the *living Christ!* When he opens up the well-spring within me, peace flows like a river. Pure motives well forth, desires after holiness, and love in its satisfying fulness. Conscience is kept clean and sweet by the presence of Christ, the fountain-head.

This fountain never dries up. It is never frozen over. No sediment defiles it. Every good thing that I ever sought for outside of Jesus Christ has had its defects, and the very best has brought a shade of disappointment. But whenever I got a deep draught of Christ's wonderful words, they were like Jonathan's honeycomb, they "enlightened my eyes." Whenever I have swallowed his promises, they have acted on me as Professor Tyndall says the canteen of fresh Swiss milk acted on him before he commenced the ascent of the Weisshorn—it lubricated his

joints and put new strength into every muscle for
the hard climb.

But we must drink from the fountain, if we
would receive strength, joy, and life. The proclamation is not, Come to the Bible and read; or,
Come to the church and listen; or, Come to the
altar and pray; or, Come to the font and be bap-
tized; or, Come to the sacramental table and partake.   It is, "Come unto ME and *drink*." This
is a voluntary act, so simple that a babe under-
stands it by instinct.   On a hot summer day we
dip the vessel into the cool spring, and, as its
delicious draught passes into the lips and through
the whole system, an exquisite refreshment steals
through every nerve and fibre of the frame.   So
doth faith take in Christ, and his grace reaches
every faculty and affection of the soul.

Coleridge said that the best proof of the inspiration of God's Word was that "it is the only
book in the world that *finds me* at every point of
my nature." The best argument for Jesus Christ
is that he alone *satisfies me*. His grace goes to
the right spot.   His comfort soothes the sore

place ; his atoning blood makes me sure of pardon ; his love cures my wretched selfishness as nothing else can do it; of almost every one and everything else we can get tired, but what true child of Christ ever got tired of the water of life? With joy doth he ever draw water from this well of salvation.

Yet tens of thousands around us are perishing, not from the want of the life-giving water, but because their foolish, depraved hearts do not thirst for it. A lady who visited one of the tropical islands for health, wrote home to her friends, "This is a lovely spot. I have every kindness, and abundance of food and fruits and luxuries, but I have no appetite. If I could only get an appetite I would soon recover." Alas, within a month she was gone ! She died, not from want of food, but from want of hunger; not for lack of refreshing drinks, but from the lack of thirst for them. So it is the worst symptom of sin in the human soul that it kills the appetite for holiness. We crave other sources of enjoyment than Christ offers. Drugged with the devil's treacherous draughts,

we cry constantly for more, and yet refuse to
touch the water of life everlasting.   Blessed are
they that thirst after purity and pardon and peace
and power; for in Christ they may be filled.

These words are written for those who are
thirsty.   Ye who have a real aspiration for a nobler and purer life, ye who have never yet been
delivered from the plague and power of sin, listen
to that celestial voice: "If any man thirst, let
him come to me and drink!"   There is a flock at
the fountain now.   Go and join them.   Draw for
yourself.   Drink for yourself.   Drink, that your
joy may be full.   In heaven there is a perpetual
Thanksgiving Day; for the Lamb who is in the
midst of the throne is their Shepherd, and he
leadeth them to ever new fountains of waters of
life.

THE GREAT PROMISE.

MANY of the sorest sorrows in this world are caused by broken promises. Oft and again the tradesman is brought to embarrassment or even bankruptcy, because the promissory notes which he held proved to be worthless. How many a home is shadowed by the sins of violated vows; hearts are broken by the broken promises of wedlock. "Till death us do part" is the solemn engagement fluently spoken, but it is the "death" of affection or of moral character that brings the real parting.

While human promises are so often broken by either wilfulness or weakness, it is a glorious thought that there is one Faithful Promiser whose word is surer than the everlasting hills. Sometimes his providence *seems* to be contradicting his promises, as when he assured Paul of the safety of all on board the corn-ship; but all in good time the shipwrecked crew and passengers escape safe to land on the broken pieces of the ship. We are often too hasty in judging our Heavenly Father, and as often mistake what he has agreed to give us. He never agrees to give us wealth or health, or freedom from care or sharp affliction. But "*this* is the promise that he hath promised us, even ETERNAL LIFE." A great deal more than deliverance from the con- demnation of sin is signified by this word "life :" it is the inbreathing of a new principle by the Holy Spirit; it is the vital organic union of the soul to the Son of God. Because he lives, we shall live also. Our whole spiritual nature is elevated, ennobled, purified, and strengthened by having this Christ-life infused. We do not lose our individuality or our responsibility to do our utmost in watchfulness or in work. The disci- ples on Galilee in the night-storm must all pull at the oars, even though Jesus was on board both as pilot and preserver. Christ's almighty grace bestows the new life, and maintains it, and most lovingly aids it; but after all, you and I must do the living. If we have only a gasping, feeble, fruitless life when he offers to give it "more abundantly," then it is our own criminal fault. We must work out our own salvation, even while he is working in us and upon us.

The real grandeur of this grand promise is that Jesus guarantees never to desert us. "My grace is sufficient for you" means all that it asserts. "No man shall be able to pluck you out of my hands" means that the hand that holds is omnipotent; all our concern must be to stay *in* that hand. We are kept by the power of God, through faith, unto salvation. A young minister, while visiting the cabin of a veteran Scotch woman who had grown ripe in experience, said to her, "Nannie, what if, after all your prayers and watching and waiting, God should suffer your soul to be eternally lost?" Looking at the youthful tyro in divinity, she replied, "Ae, dearie me, is that a' the length ye hae got to, my mon? God, let me tell ye, would hae the greatest loss. Poor Nannie wad only lose her soul, and that wad be a great loss; but God wad lose his honor and

his character. If he brak his word, he wad mak
himself a liar, and a' the universe wad gae to
ruin.''

The veteran believer was right. Our only
real ground of salvation lies in God's everlasting
word. This is the promise which he hath *promised;* let us cleave to that. If the title-deed to
my house is safely lodged in the register's office
of Brooklyn, why should I lie awake at night
for fear of ejectment from the premises? It is
my business to continue in the house, and it is
the city's business to keep secure my title to it.
Just two things are essential to a Christian's hope
of salvation. The first one is that he must be
sure that he is alive—and life is self-evidencing.
A corpse never breathes or answers questions.
As long as you really breathe out honest peni-
tence and desires after God, as long as you feel
any degree of genuine love to Jesus, as long as
your lips move in sincere prayer and your hands
move in obedience to Christ's commandment,
you are not a corpse; you are alive. The life
may be too languid and feeble, but it is there.

Make sure of that by honest self-searching, and by a comparison of yourself with what Christ demands. When your state corresponds to the Christian's state, as described in the Bible, you have the witness of the Spirit that you are his. Having this actual life, strive to have it more abundantly; the more you have, the richer, purer, stronger, and more useful you become.

Being assured that we are born again and are living to-day, the other essential is from God, and belongs exclusively to him. You and I have nothing to do with it. God will take care of his own promises. If he said, "He that believeth hath everlasting life," you have nothing to do except believe and obey. Last year I sat at eventide on the battlements of the castellated convent of Mar Saba, and looked down into the deep gorge of the Kidron. All night I lay secure in the strong fortress while the jackals howled and the Bedouin prowled without. So may every child of God who has lodged himself in the stronghold of the divine promise rest securely, and let the devil's jackals howl as loudly as they choose, or the adversary lie in wait outside the solid gateway. "This is the promise that He hath promised us, even eternal life." Cleave to that! As long as we trust God in Christ, and attest our faith by our conduct, we may roll the responsibility of our salvation upon God himself.

But will this life outlast the grave? Will it reach across that great mysterious chasm that separates us from the unseen world? Will it be *eternal?* These are the questions which sometimes torment the survivors when they have gone down to the shore of the unbridged river, and watched a beloved child or husband or wife disappear slowly out of sight. "Can I feel *sure* that there is a heaven for that loved one to land in?" But nobody comes back from that other world, nobody ever will come back, to bring a single syllable of assurance. The boats on that river of death all head one way; there are no "return trips."

Suppose that one should come back and tell us that he had actually found a heaven, and entered it, and participated in its splendors and joys. If we believed the statement, it would have to be on a single *human* authority. But if we would believe the witness of a man, is not the witness of the Almighty God infinitely greater? If we are only to feel sure of a heaven on the testimony of somebody coming back to each one of us, then would we consent to exercise a faith that glorifies a worm of the dust and dishonors the God of the universe. For one, I would rather trust a single word of *divine promise*, than a million of human assertions. Just open to the first chapter of that epistle which the Holy Spirit wrote by Peter's hand, and read the third, fourth, and fifth verses. If you, as a follower of Christ, do not feel sure of an "inheritance reserved for *you*," then you would not believe though an army of saints came back from the skies. Then *trust God!* Let your faith be

> ——"the living power from heaven
> That grasps the *promise* God has given;
> Securely fixed on Christ alone,
> Your trust shall ne'er be overthrown."

4

PATCHING THE OLD GARMENT.

———•———

SOME of our Lord's parables are to be weighed
rather than measured. Brief as to space, they
are most profound and practical in their significance. In a single verse is compressed the following parable: "No man seweth a piece of new
cloth on an old garment; else the new piece that
filled it up taketh away (or teareth away) from
the old, and the rent is made worse."

No sensible man would patch an old, thread-
bare, out-worn garment with a piece of undressed
and unfulled cloth, and for two good reasons:
the ill-matched patch would make an ugly ap-
pearance, and the strong cloth would soon tear out
from the weak, rotten fabric, and the whole process would end in failure. By this pithy parable
the Great Teacher taught that the old dispensa-
tion of ceremonial observances had had its day
and become obsolete. His gospel was a new system of religious faith and methods, entirely com-

plete and adequate for all persons and all time.
Any attempt to engraft it upon the out-worn system of Judaism would be abortive. The new
faith was to be embodied in renovated forms of
speech and forms of service.

This parable has a very practical bearing
upon the vital point of *character*, and the vital
process of *conversion*. Hardly any simile describes character better than that of a fabric,
made up of innumerable threads, and put together by numberless stitches. The earliest
stitches are commonly put in by a mother's
hand ; the subsequent work of Sunday-school
teachers and pastors may do much in the making or the marring of the fabric. A great many
poor, sleazy fabrics have a smooth and substantial
look, but in the wear of life they betray the weak
spots and ravel out. Some people also are not
stoutly sewed; they are only basted. When the
warp and woof of character is weak and worthless, when it is badly rotted by sin, there are two
methods of repair: the one is to patch up the
old; the other is to discard it altogether and pro-

cure an entirely new fabric. The first is man's plan; the second is Christ's plan. The fatal objection to the first method is that a patched character does not look well and will not last. Harmony is a prime essential of beauty, and a bright strip of virtue pieced in upon a godless life only makes the rest of the fabric look more unsightly. Nor is there strength enough in the fabric to hold the incongruous patch.

We ministers make a sad mistake when we direct our main efforts against particular sins, instead of striking at the source of all sins, a godless, unrenewed heart. Make the tree good, and the fruit will be good. Many a drunkard, disgusted and horrified by his own loathsome vice, has made a solemn resolution to break off his evil practice, but has not gone the whole length of seeking a new heart and the mighty help of God. He has attempted to patch a new habit on an old unregenerate heart. Even his temperance pledge may soon tear out and the rent be made worse. Such men as John B. Gough and Mr. Sawyer testify that what the inebriate needs is the *new fabric* wrought by the almighty power of the Holy Spirit. So with all kindred sins of falsehood, Sabbath-breaking, lechery, covetousness, and the like. A man may be shamed out of certain public acts of Sabbath desecration, and yet hide away a Sabbathless heart in his own house, and spend the day in utter defiance of God. An eloquent appeal may wring a contribution out of a stingy soul; but he will lock his purse the tighter the next time, and confirm his covetousness. What he needs is the melting power of a new affection; if he does not give from a right motive, he is none the better for having his money extorted from him. Barnabas gave his land to the Christian church because he had first given his heart to Jesus. In all my long ministry I have never been able to patch up a sinner so that he will look and act like a genuine Christian.

Christ's method of dealing with human character is the only thorough and successful method. He says, "Behold, I *make all things new.*" If any man be in Christ, and Christ in him, he is a new creature. The rotten garment has been dis-

carded, and the complete righteousness has been
put on so that the shame of his nakedness might
be hid. How sharply Jesus clove to the core of
the matter with Nicodemus ! He does not tell the
inquiring Pharisee to go home and reform certain bad habits, but "thou must be *born again.*"
The young ruler was able to display some very
bright patches of virtue, and expected to be
praised for them; but when the Saviour offered
him the entirely new garment that cost self-denial, and yet would pass him into heaven, the
poor fellow went away with his old patched robe
disappointed and sorrowful. God has ordained
this principle: that no pardon of sin and no spiritual blessing can ever be obtained except through
an inward acceptance of Christ, and an entire regeneration by the Holy Spirit. The supreme
gift of the Lord Jesus is a *new character.* The
apostles never wasted a moment on a gospel of
patchwork. Their twofold text was, "Turn to
the Lord," which meant repentance, and "Cleave
to the Lord," which meant a life of faith and
holiness.

It is quite in line with this idea of spiritual clothing that the apostle exhorts every one to "put on the Lord Jesus Christ." That signifies the entire inwrapping and infolding of ourselves in the holy texture of his perfect righteousness and all-sufficient grace. We walk inside of our clothes. So a consistent Christian walks inside of the beautiful garment which Christ has woven for him and wrapped about him. Bear in mind that it is a "seamless robe" which the dear Master provides for us; we must have it all or none. How warm it is in its ample protection against all weathers! How beautiful it is when washed white in the blood of the Lamb! How well it *wears!* I have seen it look brighter than new after fifty years of hard service, and in heaven that wedding-garment will make even a pauper to shine like an angel of light.

With such a beauty of holiness offered to us, why should so many professors of religion be content to be only a bit of shreds and patches? Certainly no unconverted worldling is ever so charmed by them as to come and say to them,

"Where did you find that? I want something just like it." Inconsistent Christians simply disgust the people of the world, and lead them to say, "If that be Christianity, I don't want it; my coat is as good as that, and better." A poor fabric is made none the better by the patchwork of public prayers or professions. A *reconversion*, a new heart-work, and a renovation of the very warp and woof of character, is what God requireth. And what a new power and beauty and irresistible influence would go forth from all our churches if we were all freshly clad in Christ Jesus!

> "This spotless robe the same appears
> When ruined nature sinks in years.
> No age can change its glorious hue;
> The robe of Christ is ever new."

A GOOD LIFE—HOW TO BEGIN IT.

SOME persons who honestly desire to begin a
better life are puzzled about the first steps. They
imagine that some intense excitement, either
within themselves, or around them in the form
of a "revival," may be indispensable. This is
a grievous mistake. Many a genuine conversion
has been attended by the anguish of a pungent
conviction of sin, and the joy of a sudden relief
and inlet of peace; but we doubt whether one-
half of the sincerest Christians have had precisely this experience. For any one to *wait* for
such an experience is folly; for any one to *demand* it from God is insane presumption.

There is one case of conversion mentioned in
the New Testament which affords a beautiful
illustration of the right way to begin a good,
honest, useful Christian life. The man himself
was not a genius, and his spiritual change had

5

nothing dramatic or "sensational" about it. He belonged to a very odious class—the tax-collectors of Palestine. The average Jew regarded the publican who wrung out of him tribute for Cæsar very much as the average "Land-Leaguer" in Ireland has regarded the British Ministry. The Jew never paid his tax without a grudge and a growl; if the publican himself were a Jew, he was excluded from the temple and from all social intercourse with his countrymen.

Our Lord, in the course of his walk from Capernaum to the country, came across one of these detested publicans sitting at the place of toll. The toll-booth was a sort of Oriental custom-house; not a permanent building, but a shed or arbor by the roadside. The collector of taxes who sat at the booth was a Jew named Levi; he is elsewhere called Matthew—a name which signifies "the gift of God." Jesus was probably no stranger to him, for every well-informed man must already have heard of the wonderful prophet from Nazareth whose words and works were the talk of all Galilee.

Christ approaches the publican kindly, and
addresses to him that short, simple sentence
which seems to have been his frequent formula
of invitation. He just said to Levi, "*Follow
me.*" That is precisely what he says to every
immortal soul through his Gospel of Love.
Christ wanted Levi—or Matthew—and Matthew
needed him. Those two brief, pithy words
changed the whole career of the publican; they
killed the old covetous self, and gave birth to
a new and noble character. We are told that
Matthew "left all, rose up, and followed" Jesus.
There was no outbreak of compunction that we
read of; certainly there was no dallying or delay.
He saw his duty; he did it.

Now what did the publican leave? Not his
property, for he soon after gave our Lord a hos-
pitable entertainment in his house. He left his
old and odious business; he left his spiritual
errors and blindness; he left his worldly aim and
his wicked heart behind. He found a new calling; he found peace of conscience; he found a
field of amazing usefulness (as a disciple and

afterwards as an inspired evangelist); he found a
Friend—and finally an everlasting inheritance
among the crowned ones in the New Jerusalem.

Here is a model for you, my friend, if you
are willing to yield to the Holy Spirit, and to
begin a new style of acting and living. Can
you make a wiser choice than Matthew made?
He was a plain, every-day man, busy at his
offensive line of work. By no means an extraor-
dinary personage like Saul of Tarsus, and by
no means awakened by a lightning-flash like the
brilliant and bloody persecutor. He did not wait
for a Pentecost, nor for any external pressure of
excitement. Neither should you. Under the
influence of a strong call from the Lord Jesus
himself, he *decided.* So can you. There was
entire free agency. Matthew was moved by the
divine love that appealed to him; his reason and
conscience were convinced; his heart was in the
step when he rose up and followed the divine
Teacher from Nazareth.

Nothing but your own stubborn, selfish, sinful will has kept you so long from accepting the

precious gift of eternal life. All the surrender
that has been required of you is to give up what
is *wrong*. All the duty that is required of you is
to do what is *right*. You must abandon your
besetting sins, and do so voluntarily. This may
cost you some struggle and self-denial, but God
will help you through. The publican "rose
up" without losing any time, or tampering with
the loving invitation. It was now or never.
Even so must your acceptance of Christ be
prompt, and your obedience be sincere and practical. Matthew did the very first thing that Jesus bade him do. Are you ready to do as much?
If not, you are rejecting Christ, and throwing
away all hope of a better, purer, safer, and holier
life.

The chief thing, observe, that the publican
did was to *follow* Jesus. He did not dictate, or
mark out a course for himself, or insist on having
his own way. He chose to go in Christ's way,
and precisely so must it be with you if you would
be a Christian in this world, and have the Christian's home in the next world. Christ goes be-

fore you; follow him.   He gives you his illuminating Word; study and obey it.   He offers you
a line of usefulness; enter it.   If he demands of
you a cross, you may so bear it as to make it a
crown.   Do not linger, I implore you.   Death
will soon find you, and cut you down in your
guilt; your last chance will be gone!   Up to
that hour at the toll-booth Matthew's life was
chaff; thenceforth it was precious wheat.   Your
life without Christ is chaff for the flames of perdition.   Listen to Jesus; obey him; follow him;
and you may open a new life whose golden grain
will be a part of the glorious harvest of heaven.

BE THOROUGH.

The bravest man of his time in Jerusalem stood up in the temple gateway, on a public occasion, and delivered a very short but a very searching sermon. It was a model of plain, pungent preaching. He did not utter any message evolved from his own brain; he gave them God's message. It ran on this wise: "All ye people of Judah, if ye will *thoroughly* amend your ways and your doings, then will I cause you to dwell in this place, in the land that I gave to your fathers." The moral condition of the people had become deplorable. The command to them is, thorough reform of character and conduct. A rich promise is made to them if they obey; if they remain wedded to their sins, their temple and their homes would be left to them desolate.

Jeremiah's pithy address to his countrymen is a capital text for our times. Wherever churches

are following the "Week of Prayer" with spe-
cial religious services for the conversion of souls,
pastors cannot go amiss in using it. President
Finney, in the days of his greatest power, used
to take such passages as this to drive them like a
plough beam-deep through the consciences of his
auditors. So he broke up the fallow ground and
got it ready for the seed of the gospel. He believed in thorough work, in a thorough exposure
of the wickedness of human hearts, in a thorough
conviction of sin, in a thorough reformation of
character under the mighty workings of the re-
newing Holy Spirit.

The fatal mistake of many people is that they
seek for a cheap religion. Some preachers and
teachers, in their desire to recommend the glorious freeness of the gospel and the simplicity of
faith, hold out the idea that it is the "*easiest*
thing in the world to become a Christian."
They hold up very attractively summer-religion,
which is all clear weather and sunshine, and
Christianity as a sort of close-covered carriage,
in which one can ride for nothing and be safely

landed, without too many jolts, at the gateway of heaven. Very little allowance is made by these rose-water teachers for the stubborn depravity of the human heart, for the tremendous power of the adversary, and for the poisonous atmosphere through which one must fight his way to the "prize of the high calling." Grand old Samuel Rutherford, in his nervous, incisive way, says, "Many people only play with Christianity, and take Christ for almost nothing. I pray you to make your soul sure of salvation, and make the seeking of heaven your daily work. If ye never had a sick night and a pained soul *for sin*, ye have not yet lighted upon Christ. Look to the right marks; if ye love him better than the world, and would quit all the world for him, then that proveth that the *work is sound.*" Probably no writer has ever combined the richest, sweetest ecstasies of devotion with a more pungent exhibition of the plainest rules of every-day morality.

The first step towards a genuine, abiding Christian character is *repentance of sin.* John

6

Baptist made this the keynote of his ministry,
which was a preparatory work for the Messiah,
just at the door. Jesus himself struck the same
note. Matthew tells us that "from that time
Jesus began to preach, and to say, Repent!"
When the apostle Peter delivered that Pente-
costal discourse which pricked into three thousand hearts, and they cried out, "What shall we
do?" his prompt answer was, "Repent!" There
is a logical necessity in this; for no man can
cleave to his sins and lay hold of Christ with the
same hand. No man can turn to the Lord until
he has turned his back upon his evil practices
and is willing to thoroughly amend his ways and
his doings. Our beloved brother Moody, indeed,
once declared that he had had far more success
when he has preached Christ's goodness than
when he has preached upon repentance; and this
reveals the only weak point we have ever discovered in the methods of this most popular and
powerful preacher of the Word. An immediate
and temporary "success" may be gained by in-
ducing a person to rise up and declare that he

believes in so lovable a being as Christ Jesus, and yet that same person may soon drift back under the dominion of the sins which he had never intelligently abandoned. We doubt whether any person ever lays thorough hold on the Saviour until he feels the need of one who can save him from his sins. Certainly no one in that death-trap of a hotel in Milwaukee even dreamed of flying to the fire-escapes until he was aroused to the dangers from the crackling flames. Why should any man betake himself to a Saviour, if he does not realize that he needs one, and that there is an abominable and deadly evil in his own heart and life that he must be saved from?

When David's eyes had been opened to behold the loathsome depravity of his own conduct, he asks for no compromise, but cries out, "Wash me *thoroughly* from my iniquity." He was ready to be thrown, like a filthy garment, into the caustic alkalies, to be rubbed and mauled and beaten until the black spots were cleansed away from the fabric. Such an abhorrence of sin it is the office of the Holy Spirit to produce; therefore should we pray for the Spirit. Such a view of his guilt it is the office of the minister to bring before every unconverted man ; therefore should the minister hold up the exceeding sinfulness of sin. The clearer the view of sin, the more thorough is likely to be the repentance. " Ye must be born again," said the Master to his anxious inquirer, Nicodemus. But the new birth, or regeneration, is the production of a new principle in us, which is antagonistic to sin as well as obedient to God.

The only evidence of repentance is thorough reformation. This takes hold both upon character and conduct; character as what we *are*, and conduct as what we *do*. This amendment must be thorough and go to the roots, or it will be as evanescent as the morning dew. The shallow "conversions" that are so often trumpeted as the result of shallow, sensational preaching, end in very shallow and short-lived religion. That dark and dismal fount-head of the *heart* is not purified by the Spirit, and pretty soon the foul streams begin to trickle out again into the daily conduct. Bad habits are not pulled up. The sharp practices are soon resumed in business transactions, or the young man soon drifts back into his convivial haunts; the unconquered bad temper begins to take fire and explode again; the covetous spirit gets hold again with a fresh grip; in short, the new emotion passes away, but it does not leave a *new man*. Christ has no hand in such conversions. They are a delusion, often an unmeasured curse. When Jesus is presented and pressed upon a sinner's acceptance, he must be presented as not only infinitely beautiful, tender, compassionate, and lovable, but as so infinitely holy that his eyes flash flame through everything *wrong*. The very bitterness of his sacrificial sufferings for us on the cross arose from the bitterness of the sin he died to atone.

One thought more. Genuine conversion demands *thorough* amendment of conduct, and no exception must be made for what we call little sins. It is not every one who is sunk, like the "City of Brussels," by one tremendous hole stoven through in an instant; small leaks, left unstopped, are equally fatal. Maclaren well says that "the worst and most fatal are often those small continuous vices which root underneath and honeycomb the soul. Many a man who thinks himself a Christian is in more danger from the daily commission, for example, of small pieces of sharp practice in his business, than ever King David was at his worst. White ants pick a carcass clean sooner than a lion will."

There is a transcendent promise that accompanies such thorough amendment of character and life. "I will let you *dwell* in this place." This bespeaks peace and permanence under the benignant smile of God. This means room to root and to grow. A soul that is rooted into Christ will thrive like a tree planted by the rivers of water; the leaves shall never wither, and death will be only a transplanting into glory.

CHRIST'S JEWELS.

THE Lord Jesus when on earth was one of the
poorest of men. He was born to poverty; he was
cradled in a stable; he went through his brief
life on foot; he had no home during his ministry
in which to lay his weary head; and his crucified
body was buried in a family tomb borrowed from
an almost stranger. Yet he was all the time laying the foundations for the most magnificent pos-
sessions in the universe of God. He was accu-
mulating the only treasures that can outlast this
fleeting globe. They are innumerable *human
souls* redeemed by him unto everlasting glory.
To them his prophetic eye looked forward when
he said, "They shall be mine in that day when
I make up my jewels." More closely rendered,
the passage is, "They shall be my *peculiar treasure* in the day I am preparing."

For one, I like the familiar phraseology in

our common version.   Christians are Christ's
jewels.   They are purchased by atoning blood;
at an infinite price was this divine ownership secured.   As the pearls are only won from the
depths of the sea by the dangerous dive of the
fishers, so were the pearls for Messiah's crown
brought up from the miry depths of depravity by
the descent of that divine Sufferer who came to
seek and to save the lost.   The most brilliant
and precious gem known to us is of the same
chemical substance as the black and opaque coal
of the mine.   Crystallization turns the carbon
into the diamond.   The grace of the Lord Jesus
transforms an opaque soul, as black by nature as
the jet, into a jewel which reflects the glory of
Christ's countenance.   All the lustre that the ri-
pest Christian character possesses is but the reflection of that Sun of Righteousness.   He who
lives nearest to Jesus shines the brightest.   A
"pearl cast before swine" is not more out of
place than is a professed follower of Jesus in the
society of scoffers or in the haunts of revelry.

Not all precious jewels glitter in conspicuous

positions. The Master has his hidden ones; there are costly sapphires beneath coarse raiment and up in the dingy attic of poverty. That self-denying daughter who wears out her youthful years in nursing a poor infirm mother is a ruby of whom the Master saith, "Thou art mine in the day when I gather my jewels." Many a precious pearl do our faithful Sunday-school teachers fish up from the dregs of ignorance into their mission-schools. From an awful depth did Jesus rescue that converted inebriate near whom we sat last Sabbath at the communion-table. All soul-saving work is a pearl-fishery for King Jesus.

"We are His workmanship," said the great apostle; and the lustre of a gem depends much on the polishing. This is often a sharp and a severe process. Many of God's people can recall the times when they were under the terrible file, or were pressed down to the grinding-wheel. Blessed be the affliction, however fierce, that gives new lustre to the diamond! The Master spendeth no time upon worthless pebbles; only

7

his jewels are polished after the similitude of a palace. Nor is this process only wrought by the divine hand; every Christian must strive to make his or her own character the more shapely and beautiful. "The roughnesses must be smoothed by careful, painstaking self-control, the untrue angles must be cut down by self-sacrifice, the surface must be evened by daily work and spiritual exercise—even trials and sorrows must be borne patiently, knowing that they will give the character an added lustre which will more worthily reflect the Master's image."

When these jewels are made ready for his many crowns, Christ will take them home unto himself. Luther said that there is great divinity in the pronouns of Scripture. "They shall be *mine*, saith the Lord." This claim is founded on the purchase made in redeeming blood. Regeneration by the Holy Spirit confirms it, and every true believer is also self-surrendered to the ownership of Christ. Up to the hour of conversion we had other proprietors—self, sin, and the devil. Now Jesus says to each Christian, Thou art

mine; I own thee. I will instruct thee, and pol-
ish thee, and put thee where it pleaseth me. I
will take care of thy salvation, and no man
shall pluck thee out of my hand. Thou shalt
be my peculiar treasure in the day of my tri-
umphant appearing. I will place thee in my
crown.

What a coronation day that will be! All
else on this globe will be but as lumber and
rubbish—fit only for the flames—in comparison
with his choice ones. Then shall the homeless
man of Nazareth come into full possession of
his magnificent trophies. The lost in hell will
be outnumbered by the saved in heaven. They
that curse Him in the pit will be far fewer
than they that crown him in the Paradise. On
the head once bleeding with the thorns will
flash the diadem of his imperial glory. And
then will all the universe confess that the ran-
som was worth all its bitter cost of agonies, when
the King shall ascend his throne of victory, and
be encircled with the constellations of his jewels.

CITIZENS OF HEAVEN.

THERE is no meaning at all in the first clause of the twentieth verse of the third chapter of Philippians—"for our conversation is in heaven"—if we use the word "conversation" in its ordinary modern sense. But if we render the sentence according to the original Greek (as it has been done in the new Revision), we have the vividly impressive truth, "Our *citizenship* is in heaven." To the Christians at Philippi this expression had a peculiar point, for Philippi was a Roman colony; Augustus had made it such after his victory over Brutus. The people were proud of the fact that they belonged to imperial Rome, and received their laws from the city of the Cæsars. While living in Philippi, their citizenship was in that proud capital which ruled the world from the banks of the Tiber.

Even so is every true child of God a citizen

of heaven. Our homestead is on high. A part
of the blood-bought family are there already,
and every day witnesses the home-coming of
thousands more. Only a thin veil separates me
from the multitudes around the throne; when
death drops the veil, I am there ! Here on earth
I am but a pilgrim—a transient lodger, for this
is not my rest. Here we who are Christ's have
no continuing city; we are seeking for and pressing towards the magnificent city that hath foundations, whose builder is the Almighty. A won-
drous comfort does this thought bring to us amid
the discomforts and the sharp trials on the road.
This life is only our training-school, to purify us
and make us more "meet" for the heavenly
community among whom we expect to dwell.

If citizens of the New Jerusalem, then our
laws come from thence. The phrase "higher
law" used to be jeered at by compromising poli-
ticians; but no statesmanship, no party, no pol-
icy can stand the test which is not conformed
to God's everlasting law of right. The best citizens of this republic are those whose lives are

loyal to the higher law which God has written
in his Word. No statute is fit to be enacted
which contravenes God's truth; and that professed Christian is a coward and a traitor to his
Master who does not carry his religion into his
politics as much as into his business pursuits or
his household.

"If ye love me," said our loving Redeemer,
"keep my commandments." The world around
us has its unwritten code of morals and of man-
ners. It sets up its standards and fixes its fashions to suit itself. But they are no rule for you
and me; Jesus has "chosen us out of the world,"
and given his own life to be our standard and
our pattern. Every consistent Christian's motto
should be: I must live *for* this world, and yet not
be *of* it. Daniel did his best service for wicked
Babylon by keeping his windows open towards
Jerusalem, and by loyalty to its everlasting King.
This world never will be converted by conformity to it; but it would be overwhelmingly im-
pressed by the sight of a vast body of people who
should live and speak and act as the *citizens of*

heaven itself. What a salt would our influence be; what a power would our example be; what a trumpet our every word!

Every Christian, therefore, should dare to be singular. It is of little account to be judged of man's judgment; he who judgeth us is the Lord. We are members of society, and bound to contribute our very utmost to its benefit; but we do that best by remembering that our first allegiance is to that society whose leader is Christ. *We report to headquarters.* The first question with me as a Christian is, What does my Master command? Would he approve my mode of doing business, my style of living, my amusements, my temper, my whole daily conduct? If so, that is enough. My citizenship is with him, and I must see to it that other people recognize that fact. I am not "to be had" when sinful customs make their claims, or worldly seductions offer their bribes.

If I am Christ's servant, then I am a citizen of no mean city—a member of no mean family. Let every Christian assert his high birth by his

high bearing.   He is never to stoop to anything
low, never to be caught at contemptible tricks,
never found in suspicious places.   As high as
the heavens are above the earth, so much higher
should a Christian's ways and words and whole
conduct be above the ways of sinners.   He should
never "apologize" to the world for daring to do
right.

If we are citizens of heaven, let us be ever
setting our affections on things above, on the
treasures that are laid up at His right hand.
Just as surely as we set our hearts on any lower
objects, our hearts are apt to be *broken.*   But
when I climb high enough to put my heart, my
aims, my most treasured things in the keeping
of my Saviour, then Satan himself cannot reach
them.   Is not this the true "higher life," after
all?

The amazing grandeur and glory of this citizenship of heaven will be fully realized when
we get there.   John says that once "there was
silence in heaven for the space of half an hour."
Surely if you or I reach the Celestial City, and

are ushered into its transcendent light and rush of melodies, we may well be struck silent with unutterable wonder that we are there. Yet we *shall* be there, if we secure our title through Christ's atoning blood, and if we walk worthy of our high calling, and if we endure as seeing him who is invisible. Then we colonists on this planet shall go home to our *mother country*, and be for ever with our King!

GIVE CHRIST THE BEST.

"THE *best* is always good enough for me," was the playful reply of a lady friend of ours when we asked her which of several things she would prefer. What our friend said playfully may be applied in all seriousness to the gifts which every Christian ought to offer to his Redeemer. The best is never too good for him; in fact, we should never put off our Lord with anything less.

The primal idea of true Christianity is this giving to Jesus all we have and all we are. This is one important meaning of that much-perverted word *sanctification*. Some people use it to signify a process of purification, or a putting off of moral filthiness, until a perfect sinlessness is reached. But the ordinary meaning of "sanctify" is to set apart, to consecrate to God. When Jesus said, "I sanctify myself," he certainly did not affirm

that he was putting off impurity and becoming
perfectly holy. He had never been anything
else than sinless. He intended to say, "I *consecrate* myself to the redemption of man and the
fulfilment of my Father's will." A true Chrîs-
tian life is the continual consecration of our bodily powers, of our energies, our affections, our
money, our influence to Him who bought us
with his blood. The more willing we are to give
Jesus the very best we have, the more nearly are
we attaining to genuine holiness. Is this the
usual practice of those who profess and call themselves Christian ?

Take the matter of money. How many
Christians habitually give a due share of their
income to the Lord? "Ah, I cannot afford to
give so much as I once did," is a very current
apology. Yes; but you have not retrenched in
your style of living. You began by cutting down
in your contributions to benevolence, when that
ought to have been the very last thing to be
touched when retrenchment was forced upon
you. The true principle is, give God the first

claim, and let others wait until he has been
served. "When I get any money," said Eras-
mus, "I buy books; if any is left I buy clothes."
There spoke the genuine scholar.

But too many Christians say in practice, "If
I am making money, I shall treat myself to a new
carriage, or my family to new furniture, etc.; if
there is anything over, I will put it in the contri-
bution-box." The fattest sheep is killed for the
table of selfishness. The poor "crow-bait" is
palmed off for sacrifice upon God's altar. This
same wretched principle is manifested when six
days are given to business, and one or two evening hours are stingily begrudged to the prayer-
meeting or to works of benevolence. The pun-
ishment of all such petit larceny of the Lord is
that the perpetrators become mere "crow-baits"
spiritually, and never taste the rich morsels which
God bestows. "The liberal soul shall be made
fat;" all the rest are but skin and bone.

Here is a solemn question for parents in
training their children, and for Christian sons
and daughters in choosing their calling. "That

boy is a very bright fellow; I will make a law-
yer of him.   His brother is a good conscien-
tious chap ; but he has brains enough, I think,
for a parson." So reasons the *pater familias*,
and the sons catch the infection.   The one with
ten talents goes to the Bar, and perhaps becomes a great advocate and a very small Christian.   The one with two talents consecrates them
to the work of winning souls, and becomes the
heir of a great inheritance in heaven.   God
blessed the one who gave him the best he had;
. the other "reaped where he had sowed," and
did not get a basketful.

Jesus Christ has a sovereign right to the best
brains, the best culture, the best estates, the best
powers in the land.   Suppose that the venerable
Stephen H. Tyng had decided in his youth that
his capacities were only worthy of the Bar or the
Senate House.   Suppose that he had entered the
lists for wealth and fame, and climbed to the
highest round of the ladder.   When the frosts of
fourscore were gathering on his brow, would he
have been the happy man he has been, with the

benedictions of Heaven covering his gray hairs like a crown of light?

We do not affirm that a man cannot serve Christ in any other calling than the ministry. But we do affirm that self should never be consulted by a true Christian in making life's choices. Christ's prior right to the very best is the only right rule. And that rule, well observed, will give to Christ's service the "pick" of human power and influence. What is left over may go to the inferior claims of "the things that perish."

RIGHT AND WRONG PRAYING.

"FIND thy happiness in God, and he shall give thee the askings of thy heart." This is the exact rendering of the fourth verse of the thirty-seventh Psalm, and it throws a flood of light upon the important question of what is right and what is wrong prayer. A great deal of prayer is born of selfishness, and takes on the airs of dictation to our Heavenly Father. It is not humble supplication, born of a devout, submissive spirit; but it amounts to a demand. When we go into our bank and present a check for one thousand dollars, we have a right to demand that sum from the paying-teller, provided that sum stands to our credit on the books of the institution. But God's promises to his children are not unconditional; and we have no such spiritual assets standing to our credit that we may presume to dictate to the God of wisdom and of love.

The hackneyed illustration of "drawing on the bank of faith" may be very misleading. What is laid down distinctly as the indispensable quality of right asking in the above quoted verse from the Psalm? It is a *right feeling towards God*. When a soul comes into such an entire submissiveness towards God that it can honestly say, "Not as I will, but as thou wilt;" when that soul delights in seeing God reign, and in seeing his glory advanced, then its desires will be so purified and so strained from the dregs of selfishness that they may be fearlessly poured out before God. In this frame of unselfish submissiveness the soul may indeed come boldly to the throne of grace, and ask for grace suited to its every hour of need. The desires of God and the desires of a sincere Christly soul will *agree*. God loves to give to them who love to let him have his way. They are as willing to accept his "no" as his "yes," for they are seeking not their own glory, but his; they find their happiness in the chime of their own desires with the will of God.

A capital illustration of the difference between right and wrong desires is furnished in the biographies of James and John. These two fisher-men-disciples come to our Lord and say to him, "Master, we would thou shouldst do for us whatsoever we shall desire." Then bolts out the amazing request that he would place one of them on his right hand and the other on his left, when he set up his imperial government at Jerusalem or elsewhere. Disguise it as they might, they were selfish office-seekers. Their dream was of twelve thrones, with their own in the centre; his foresight saw instead of this three crosses of agony and shame, his own in the centre. It was not a crown, but a cup of suffering, that was in preparation, and he tenderly inquires if they were ready for that. As long as those two ambitious disciples found their happiness in self-seeking, Jesus would not and could not give them the askings of their hearts.

Now, look on a few years farther, and you will find those two identical men uttering the strongest declarations in behalf of God's willing-

9

ness to hear and answer prayer. Their own hearts have been so renewed by the Holy Spirit, they have become so consecrated to their Master's service, and they are in such complete chime with him, that they are not afraid to come to him and say, "Do for us what we desire." Having purified and unselfish desires, they rejoice to discover how fully and delightfully they are satisfied—even more abundantly than they asked. So one of them (James) declares that if any of us lack wisdom we must ask of God, who giveth liberally. And then—as if he remembered what a disgracefully selfish prayer he had once been guilty of—he says, "Ye ask and ye receive not, because ye *ask amiss*, that ye may consume it upon your own pleasures." The other disciple (beloved John) exclaims, "Whatsoever we ask we receive of him, *because* we keep his commandments, and do those things that are pleasing in his sight." It is not self any longer that is to be pampered, but God that is honored. Just as soon as those two Christians found their supreme happiness in Christ and his cause, they received the askings of their hearts. Christ and they were at one. As a kind father loves to grant the reasonable requests of a dutiful son, so does our Heavenly Father love to grant righteous and reasonable requests through Jesus, the Intercessor.

The only "prayer-gauge" I believe in is that which gauges the character of our prayers and the spirit in which we offer them. The very first essential to all right prayer is unconditional submissiveness to God's will. "Nevertheless, Father, not as I will, but as thou wilt." The richest blessing that prayer can bring is to bring us into closer communion and agreement with the all-holy and the all-loving One. Dr. Bushnell's illustration of the "bow-line" represents this most happily. A man stands in the bow of the boat, and draws upon a line attached to the shore. His pull does not move the solid ground one hair's breadth, but it does move his boat towards the land. So when I attach the line of my desire fast to the everlasting throne, faith does not expect to move the throne, but to draw

me closer to it; and when I get more and more
into harmony with God, I receive what my heart
most desires. Finding my happiness in Christ,
I am satisfied. Money, health, promotion, ease,
and all kindred cravings, are only lawful when
they are subordinated to the higher love; and
the moment they get the upper hand we must
expect to be dismissed as John and James were
when self got the upper hand in them.

The question now arises, What are right desires? As far as my ignorance has been enlightened by the Word, I would reply that every desire is a right one which aims only to please
God and not self. Grace does not forbid desires,
or reduce us to a spiritual emasculation. It en-
courages at the same time that it purifies and
directs our desires. Nay, the Bible exhorts us to
"desire spiritual gifts." Wisdom from above,
strength for the hour of need, faith, the outpour-
ing of the Holy Spirit, and kindred blessings,
are in harmony with God's promises. These
are the very things he has told us to covet. For
them we are to "open our mouths wide" and

our hearts; and when we do this we are filled
unto all the fulness of God.   Our Heavenly
Father does not hand over to us the reins when
our selfishness grasps after them.   Nor does he
allow our ignorance to be the judge of what is
best for us.   He often surprises us by sending
something better than what we petitioned for.
But infinitely the best thing which he can give
us is *his favor, which is life.*   If we find our supreme happiness in this—oh, how our souls are
purified of low, selfish, wayward, and wicked
desires; and with what banqueting on his love,
and with what foretastes of heaven, our best askings are answered !

THE NIGHT OF FAILURE—THE MORNING OF FAITH.

———•———

MANY of the personal incidents in the lives of our Lord and his disciples light up, like transparencies, with vivid spiritual instruction. One of these is in that most suggestive experience of Peter and Andrew and the two sons of Zebedee, when they "toiled all the night" with their nets and drew in nothing. That long night's work— and probably hard work too—meant failure. Peter's sad words, "Master, we have toiled all night and taken nothing," might be written under the history of more than one human undertaking. Pastors sometimes write this epitaph over their sermons, or over a period of labor that ends in empty nets. Reformers—looking at the largeness of outlay and expectations, and the smallness of visible results—have often thrown away their nets in sheer despair.

Say what we may, the fact remains that good
men and women who toil hard in a noble undertaking do not always win immediate success—
none certainly that is visible to their own eyes.
God is a sovereign. And that signifies that God
always means to have his own way, and not ours.
We may man our prayer services, or our mission
enterprises, or any other Christian undertakings,
with a boat-load of capable workers, and just as
sure as we begin to count our fish before we have
caught them, we may come to shore at last with
an empty net. "Not by might, nor by power,
but by my Spirit, saith the Lord of hosts." Even
Paul's arm may swing the seed-bag, and Apollos
may guide the irrigating water with his foot, but
God alone can give the increase. This is the lesson which we have to be taught again and again;
for our Heavenly Father always vetoes every
claim of human independence.

But let us turn over the leaf and see how the
night of failure was followed by the morning of
faith. When the sun had lighted up the blue
waves of Galilee, and a whole navy of fishing-

boats are lying by the strand, Jesus appears. He
delivers a discourse to the multitude on the beach,
and then he bethinks him of his poor, disappointed disciples. He always feels for us in our disap-
pointments. Knowing what a tedious and fruitless night the four fishermen had spent, and seeing
that their nets were washed and mended, he gave
the order, "Launch out into the deep, and let
down your nets for a draught." Peter had a vast
deal of human nature in him; so he frankly says,
"Master, we have toiled all night and taken nothing." Had he stopped there, he would have de-
served a sharp rebuke. He was despondent, but
he was not despairing. So out bolts from his
eager tongue that noble answer, "Nevertheless,
Lord, at thy word I will let down the net." Here
is a motto for faith to nail to its masts. Faith is
more than willing to try another venture—yes, a
score of them—provided that it has the "word"
of Jesus for going ahead. Christ offered to go
with them himself. Christ gives the word of
command, "Launch out into the deep !" Faith
has nothing to do but obey orders and bend to the

oar. Down goes the net. And lo! a mighty
swarm of fish is pouring into the net, so that the
meshes are breaking with the strain. As busy as
fervent Christians are in the most glorious revival are Peter and Andrew in hauling in that overloaded net. Ah, faith has brought FULNESS now.
It always does. Peter makes signal to John and
James to bring their two smacks alongside and to
help harvest the multitude of fish. Both boats
are so overloaded that they are in danger of sink-
ing. And Peter is so overwhelmed with the mi-
raculous power of Jesus of Nazareth that he
throws himself down at Jesus' knees, and cries
out, "O Lord, I am a sinful man!" So grand
does Jesus seem to him, and so mean does he seem
to himself, that he does not feel fit to remain in
his Lord's presence. Sweet indeed was Christ's
reply to the awe-struck disciple, "Fear not, Peter; henceforth thou shalt fish for souls; henceforth thou shalt catch *men.*"

I have often thought that the experience of
that night of failure and that forenoon of success
must have been a capital lesson in the schooling

10

of those apostles. Just such a lesson we need now. We need to be taught that success does not depend on strong arms or strong nets or well-manned boats. It depends on Christ's presence with us in the boats, and our obeying his divine directions.

Methinks that we hear his heavenly voice of love saying to all of us, brothers and sisters, "Launch out into the deep !" Leave the shallow places. Seek for deep experience—deep study of God's precious truth—and deeper draughts of the Spirit of Christ. Then we cannot utterly fail; for faith overcometh, and all things are possible to him that believeth. At the end of every night spent without Christ (however hard we toil) you may write "failure." At the close of every day spent with Christ, and under his oversight, you will joyfully write, " fulness of blessings."

CHRISTIANS FOR THE WORLD—NOT OF IT.

THERE was a prodigious significance in that intercessory prayer of our Lord on the eve of his sufferings: "I pray not that thou shouldst take them out of the world, but that thou shouldst keep them from the evil." The preservation of the world from moral ruin depended on the preservation of the church of God. "Ye are my witnesses," said the Master. The followers of Christ were to be his representatives; the visibility of Christ on earth was to be in the persons, in the acts and lives of those whom he had redeemed to be a peculiar people, zealous in good works. They were to be a wholesome leaven, penetrating the whole mass of humanity; they were to be the salt of the earth, preserving society from putrefaction by the savor of pure godliness. "Let your light shine!" To "shine" means something more than the possession of a renewed heart or the enjoyment of an inward peace. It signifies the luminous reflection of Christ in character and conduct.

This world cannot afford to have Christians degenerate or become demoralized. No city can afford to have its gas apparatus so damaged as to leave its streets in darkness, or its sanitary system so neglected as to leave it a prey to typhoid fevers or cholera. Divine grace is imparted in order to purify its possessor; and he, in turn, is to do his part to purify the community. If he fails, the community is the loser. We who profess to call ourselves Christians ought to know that the world expects us to stand for righteousness, and never to compromise; to act as disinfectants and to maintain our savor; to hold them up, and not to be dragged down by them. If all the Christianity in existence were to become bankrupt in character, even the scoffers themselves would be frightened. Sneer as they may, they expect us to stand by our colors. Our desertion of God and of the right would not only disgrace us; it would alarm even the ungodly. "If this world is so bad with the Christian religion," said the shrewd Franklin, "what would it be without it?"

A personal incident will illustrate this secret reliance which the people of the world have upon the people of God. A young man, who was a professed Christian, was seeking to win the heart and hand of a young lady of wealth and fashion. His suit did not prosper, and one day she said to him, "You know that you are a church member, and I am a gay girl, very fond of what you call the pleasures of the world." This led him to suspect that his religion was the obstacle to his success in winning her consent to marry him. He accordingly applied to the officers of his church, which must have been very loose in its joints, for a release from his membership. They granted it. "Now," said he to her, when he met her again, "the barrier is removed. I have withdrawn from my church and I do not make any profession to be a Christian." The honest-hearted girl turned on him with disgust and horror, and said to him, "M——, you know that I have led a frivolous life, and I feel too weak to resist temptations. I determined that I never would marry any man who was not strong enough to stand firm himself, and to hold me up also. I said what I did *just to try you;* and, if you have not principle enough to stick to your faith, you have not principle enough to be my husband. Let me never see you again.''

Whether this incident be actual or not, the lesson it teaches is beyond dispute. The world expects Christians to stand by their colors; when we desert them, we not only dishonor our Master and ourselves, but we disappoint the world. Christ's church never will save the world by secularizing itself or surrendering its strict principles of loyalty to whatever is right and pure and holy. Conformity to the world will never convert it. '' Come out and be ye separate,'' saith the Lord, ''and touch no unclean thing.'' Even if the world could succeed in bringing the church down to its own standard of opinion and practice, it would only work its own moral destruction. It would extinguish the light-houses which illu-

mine its own channels; it would destroy the
spiritual leaven which Christ has ordained and
prepared to save human society from corruption.

The demand of this time is not to lower the
claims of God, but to elevate them; not to weak-
en the authority of divine inspiration, but to re-
inforce it; not to unloose obligations to Bible
creeds, but to tighten; not to accommodate Christianity to the thought and fashion of the times,
but to keep it stoutly and steadily up to its primitive standards. We must stand fast not only to
the faith once delivered to the saints, but to the
practices enjoined in God's Word. The church
of this day is in no danger of excessive Puritan-
ism. The peril is in the opposite direction.
Conformity to the world is weakening the back-
bone of the church, and thus far diminishing its
power to lift the world up towards God. "If
thou wouldst pull a man out of a pit," said
quaint old Philip Henry, "thou must have a
good foothold, or else he will pull thee in."

In no direction should Christians make their

testimony more emphatic than in the line of righteous living. The sin of modern civilization has been well described as "making more of *condition* than it does of *character*." The very essence of Bible religion is to make character everything, and conduct the test and evidence of character. "By their fruits ye shall know them;" make the tree good and the fruits shall be like it. This is the core of Christ's practical teachings. He "gave himself for us, that he might redeem us from all iniquity and purify unto himself a peculiar people." The Revised Version has it "that he might purify unto himself a people for his own possession." The gist of this is that Christ owns us, and not the world. Our first duty is to him, and really this is the most effectual way of serving them. Our loyalty to Christ is to be the world's salvation. The moment we betray him we betray them and empty ourselves of all reforming and regenerating power. When the salt has lost its savor it is thenceforth good for nothing but to be cast out and trodden under foot of men. When a Christian so conducts himself as to be despised by his unconverted neighbors, he inflicts upon them an incalculable injury. He confirms them in unbelief. He brings Christianity into contempt. He poisons the well from which they ought to draw good influences. "Ye are my witnesses," said our loving Lord and Master; but what if the witnesses *swear falsely?*

In whatever direction we apply it, the fact remains clear that society needs a strict, pure, honest, self-denying, godly-minded church. Our politics need a chloride of lime; and Christian citizens ought to engage in civil affairs, not to become tainted themselves, but to purify civil life. To a right-minded Christian a ballot is a trust, and public office is a stewardship for God. The most grievous calamity that could happen to this country would be a divorce of practical Christianity from its politics. Conscience is more to this republic than all its army or navy, or millions of Government bonds.

In commerce and trade Christianity has its indispensable place, and God's people their sphere of usefulness. The Golden Rule is the true Christian's yardstick; commerce becomes a cheat if it is disused or broken. When a church member defaults or turns swindler, he repeats the sin of Judas. Christ is betrayed, and men's faith in Bible integrity is so far shattered. A Christian merchant, manufacturer, or mechanic has a call to serve Christ and save his fellow-men as much as any gospel minister. Every ounce of leaven has its place.

Social life, with increase of wealth, has a trend towards demoralization. Luxury enervates. Popular amusements become sensualized and offer their temptations to the church. " Be ye not conformed to the world" applies to the stage, the ball-room, the wine-cup, and to everything that would turn God's earth into a " Vanity Fair." Conformity to the world amounts, in the end, to more than the corruption of Christ's church. It puts out the light which Christ kindled; it destroys the very leaven which he has prepared to purify and sweeten and save a " world lying in wickedness."

A SERMON ALL THE WEEK.

"WHY do you go to hear Dr. A—— preach?
He is not a brilliant preacher." "Very true,"
was the sensible reply; "I know that his pulpit
performances are not brilliant, but his *life* is a
sermon to me all the week." With a minister,
as much as with the private Christian, character
tells. More than one pulpit orator has destroyed
the effect of his discourses by his self-seeking
egotism, or his unscrupulous practices, or his
overbearing temper, or some other very unchris-
tian trait. On the other hand, full one-half of
the power of some eminent pastors lies in their
pure, unblemished piety. Everybody believes
in them. Their unselfish humility would silence
a scoffer. Good as they are in the pulpit, they
are still better out of it. Their life is eloquent
from Monday morning to Saturday night.

What is true of the ministry is equally true of

the laity. An honest, consistent, godly character
is a "sermon all the week." Nay, it is Christ's
own preaching; for Christ liveth in such a believer, and shines out from him. This good
man's fruits are Christ's fruits, just as much as
the big, luscious grapes are the outcome of a
"Hamburg" vine. The credit does not belong
to the grapes so much as it belongs to the vine
which yields such superb fruit. Our divine Lord
recognized this when he said that herein was he
glorified when his disciples bore much fruit.

The living Christian—pure of heart and unspotted by the world—is the best preacher of the
gospel in these days. And it is just from the
lack of this gospel salt that society suffers corruption and decay. Revivals and conversions
are painfully few. The revival that is most ur-
gently needed is a revival of *practical godliness.*
Sunday preaching is not enough ; we want more
"sermons all through the week."

Let us go down to the core. The only basis
of good character is a renewed heart, a heart in
which Jesus Christ lives by his divine Spirit, a

heart which is in the habit of obeying Christ's commandments. Such a man draws his motives of action from his deep, abiding love to Jesus. Up from the very roots comes his daily devotion to those things which are pure and honest and lovely and of good report. Rooted into Christ, he is not easily shaken. He does not bend to trickery or yield to temptation. The world cannot move such a man. What cares he for its changing, frivolous fashions; his fashion is to do the will of his holy Master.

A spiritual drought does not dry up such a Christian. Some church members are only flourishing during the heavy rains of a revival season; the rest of the year they are as brown and barren as the plains of Nevada. If their pastors grow sick and tired of such fitful professors, how patient must their Lord be to endure them at all!

Let the reader of this volume examine himself, or herself, in the light of conscience and God's Word. Perhaps you are wondering why so few are converted, and why the church has so little power, and why the attendance upon God's house is so scanty, and the state of religion is so low. The reason is that more of the *preaching* of *practice* is needed all through the week. And none of us can rise higher before the world than the fountain-head in our *own hearts.* "O God, renew within me a right spirit!"

THE LILY-WORK ON THE PILLARS.

THERE were two massive pillars in the porch
of Solomon's Temple which bore the names of
"Jachin" and "Boaz." One name signifies
"He will establish," and the other signifies "In
strength." The two together are admirable em-
blems of solid goodness of character. Not hol-
low, not easily thrown off their base, and of un-
decaying material, they typify the firmness and
the strength of the man who is immovably fixed,
trusting on the Lord. But, while these two pillars were made strong, they were also made orna-
mental; for they were inwreathed with delicate
chains of carved pomegranates, and "upon the
capitals of the pillars *was lily-work*." Thus are
strength and beauty to be combined in every
well-developed Christian character.

Beauty is that combination of harmony in
color or in form that gives pleasure to the eye of

the beholder. One of the profoundest prayers in the Bible is the prayer that the beauty of the Lord our God may be upon us. One of the richest promises is that "the meek will He beautify with salvation," and the loftiest ideal set before us is "the beauty of holiness." When our eyes gaze upon our enthroned Saviour in his celestial splendors, then shall they "see the King in his beauty." It was the ineffable perfection of Jesus of Nazareth which not only constitutes the glory of the New Testament, but furnishes the most unanswerable argument for the essential divinity that was clothed in human form.

Christ enjoined upon every one of his disciples to study him, to learn of him, and to imitate his example. A true Christian is the representative of Christ in this world—the only embodiment of gospel teaching and influences that is presented in human society. How vitally important is it, then, that those of us who profess and call ourselves Christians should make our Christianity *attractive!* Multitudes of people know very little and think very little about the Lord Jesus; nearly all the ideas they get of his religion is what they see in those who profess it, and their eyes are as sharp as those of a lynx to discover whether their neighbor is one whit the better for his religion. I will venture to say that the life of William E. Dodge was the most eloquent sermon in behalf of practical Christianity which has been presented in this community lately. It was worth many a volume of ingenious Apologetics to refute infidelity and silence the gainsayers.

But not all the solid piety is as attractive as it might be made. There is many a Jachin and a Boaz that has not much lily-work about his harsh and repulsive character. Of course we do not refer to such disgraceful delinquencies as some church members are guilty of, who defraud their neighbors, or steal trust funds, or practise knaveries in politics, or befoul themselves with sensual excesses. Such members of the flock do not wear a fleece big enough to hide the wolf. But we might instance thousands of genuine Christians, honest at heart and sincere in their professions, who would be wonderfully improved by lopping off some of their unsightly branches. Egotistical brother A—— would look better in the eyes of his neighbors if he had not so many "I's" of his own. Brother B—— is devout in his prayers, but his clerks and his employés would enjoy hearing them better if he did not treat them as if they were pack-mules. Mrs. C—— is indefatigable in the Ladies' Benevolent Union; but her ill-conditioned children look as if they needed a Dorcas Society at home. And so we might go through the alphabet with descriptions of those whom the grace of God has converted, but they have not added many of the graces of "lily-work" to their religious constructions.

None of us need travel a mile to find some unquestionable Christians who sour their religion with censoriousness. Grant that their standard is high and exacting; but who made them judges over their neighbors? After an hour's talk with them, you acquire an insensible prejudice against some of the best people in your community. Such Christians are in God's orchard; but they

bear crab apples. Everybody respects their sin-
cerity, both in creed and conduct; yet nobody
loves them. I once had a venerable and most
godly-minded member of my church who never
did a very wrong act to my knowledge. I am
sorry to say that he scarcely ever did a pleasant
one. There was a good, sound nut in that chest-
nut-burr; but no one liked to prick his fingers in
coming at it. So the rugged, honest old man
(who in a humble way reminded me of Carlyle)
was left to go on his way to heaven, working
and praying and scolding as he went stubbornly
along; and even the children in the street were
almost afraid to speak to him. I suppose he has
grown mellower since he passed into the genial
atmosphere of the better world. One of the most
blessed things about heaven is that the best and
holiest who are admitted there will have left
every disagreeable thing about them outside the
gates.

Sanctification is a genuine and gracious process, and it never reaches completeness in this
life. This should make us tolerant and charita-

ble towards the infirmities of sincere followers of our Master. Yet it should never excuse our own wilful adherence to words, or practices, or traits of character which disfigure our religion and mar our influence. In building a character for eternity we should regard its impression on our fellow-men; we are as much bound to ornament it with the "lily-work" as we are to make the structure solid and enduring. An attractive Christian is the one who hits the most nearly that golden mean between pliant laxities on the one hand and severe or sanctimonious harshness on the other hand. He is strict, but not censorious. He is sound, and yet sweet and mellow, as one who dwells much in the sunshine of Christ's countenance. He never incurs contempt by compromising with wrong, nor does he provoke others to dislike of him by doing right in a very harsh or hateful or bigoted fashion.

Our Master is our model. What marvellous lily-work of gentleness, forbearance, and unselfish love adorned the massive divinity of that life! What he was, we, in our imperfect meas-

ure, should pray and strive after.   Study Jesus,
brethren.   Get your souls saturated with his
spirit.   His grace imparted to you and his example imitated can turn deformity into beauty,
and adorn your lives with whatsoever things are
true and honest and lovely and of good report.
He that winneth souls is wise.   But if we would
win the careless and the godless to our Saviour,
we must make our daily religion more winsome.

STANDING THE STRAIN.

How often do we ever hear a sermon or ever think about poor Rizpah ? There she sits—in the sacred story—for five long, weary months upon the sackcloth spread on the rock of Gibeah. The noonday sun pours down its heats upon her head, and the midnight its chilling dews, but they cannot drive her from her steady vigil beside the forms of her two crucified sons. From the early harvests of April to the early rains of October she suffers neither the birds of the air to assail them by day, nor the beasts of the field by night. The wayfarers by the northern road from Jerusalem grow accustomed to the strange, sad spectacle of that heart-broken mother guarding from vulture and jackal the remains of her beautiful Mephibosheth and Armoni.

Those two youths were crucified; there seems but little doubt of that. They were sacrificed to

appease the wrath of the Gibeonites for the cruel-
ties once practised upon them by the hands of
their father Saul. If we could ask that long-
enduring woman, Rizpah, what enabled her to
stand those five months of severe strain, her answer would be in one single word, "*Love.*" It
was the quenchless affection of a true mother's
heart. It transcends every other earth-born affection. It can neither be "chilled by selfishness,
nor daunted by danger, nor weakened by worth-
lessness, nor stifled by ingratitude." This was
the chord that bound Rizpah to that long vigil
on the desolate rock and stood the tremendous
strain.

There is a lesson for every Christian in this
touching episode of the "*mater dolorosa*" on the
rock of Gibeah. There is only one principle in
the human heart which can withstand the severe
strain which the daily wear and tear of temptation and trial bring upon us. It is *love for Jesus.*
Our heart must be in our religion, and our religion in our heart, or else it is a most toilsome
drudgery or an irksome hypocrisy. This is the

secret reason why so many church members shirk
their duties. There is no genuine, long-enduring
love of their crucified Master at the core of the
heart. So their religion is toil and task-work.
The Bible is taken as a medicine, and not de-
voured as honey. There must be a constant
baiting and bribing by attractions of fine preaching and fine music, or else the Sabbath service
would be a sort of compulsory penance. As it
is, about every rainy Sunday brings doubt and
disgrace upon full one-half of the professed piety
of the land. A man in whose soul love for Jesus
rings no bell of devotion is always glad of an excuse to shirk the sanctuary on a disagreeable day.
Money-giving for Christ's cause is to such a professor an orthodox larceny; he flings his contribution at the box grudgingly, as if he would say,
" There it is, since you must have it; when will
these everlasting calls be done with?" The
whole routine of external service in the name of
religion is gone through slavishly, perfunctorily,
and heartlessly, as if the lash of an overseer was
brandished over the head. Such Christianity is

Christless. There is no joy and no power in it, and when a severe strain of temptation comes on its possessor, it snaps like a thread, and leaves him to a terrible fall. The secret of every case of bad backsliding during the past year has been the want of *staying* power; and that staying power is based solely on the indwelling of Christ and a supreme love for him.

Love of Jesus is essential Christianity. It endureth all things; it never faileth. No privations can starve it, and no burdens can break it down. It keeps the heart of the frontier missionary warm amid the snows of the Rocky Mountains, and gives sweetness to the crust which the overworked seamstress eats in her lonely lodging—disdaining the wages of sin. It is the core of *all* the piety which Christ loves to look at. It is the only cure also of the reigning worldliness and covetousness and fashion-worship which have made such spiritual havoc in too many churches.

The test-question for every Christian life is, Have I in my inmost heart a love of Jesus strong enough to *stand the strain?* My religious profession has lost its novelty; will it hold out? Temptations will come; shall I conquer them or break? Christ demands constant loyalty; can I be true to him? Am I as ready to stand watch day and night to protect his honor as poor Rizpah was to protect the lifeless forms of her beloved from the birds and the beasts? These are the questions that touch the very marrow of our religion. They underlie all our heart-life, our church-life, and the very existence of every work of self-denying charity.

My brother, there is only one way to be a *staying* Christian, a thorough soul-saving Christian. It is to get the heart full of Jesus—so full that the world and the lusts of the flesh and the devil can get no foothold. Whether you are a pastor longing for a fresh blessing on your flock, or a Sabbath-school teacher set in charge of young immortals, or a parent guarding the fireside fold, or a philanthropist toiling for the ignorant, the suffering, and the lost, you need this ever-living mainstay and inspiration. If you

only love Jesus, you will love to live for him and
to labor for him. Jacob toiled seven years faith-
fully for Rachel, and they seemed unto him but
a few days, for the love which he had to the
beautiful maiden in the fields of Laban. Love's
labors were light. Would you then be a light-
some, joyous laborer in Christ's vineyard? Get
your heart full of him. Would you be a power
in your church? Get the heart full of Jesus.
Would you be kept safe from backsliding? Then
keep yourself in the love of your Saviour. Put
that master-affection so deep down that it shall
underlie all selfishness; so deep that the frosts of
the current skepticism cannot reach it; so deep
that the frictions of daily life cannot wear upon
it; so deep that the power of temptation cannot
touch it; so deep that even when old age dries
up the other affections of our nature, this undy-
ing love shall flow like an artesian well.

Let us stop then occasionally and take one
look at that steadfast Rizpah watching beside the
crosses of her crucified sons. She *stood the strain*,
until her noble constancy won the king's eye and

secured their honorable burial. There is an infinitely holier cross, an infinitely diviner Sacrifice
that demands our steadfast loyalty. If a mother's
love could endure so much, what will not the love
of a redeemed soul bear for its Redeemer? Oh, for
a fresh baptism of this mighty love—a fresh and
a full inpouring, so that no accursed spirit of the
world, no temptation, no self-indulgence, no, nor
any other creature, shall be able to *separate* us
from the love of God which is in Christ Jesus our
Lord!

TURNING WINTER INTO SPRING.

——•——

At the midwinter season many people fall, naturally, into the error that the sun emits less heat than during the midsummer. But while we are shivering with the cold, the fact is that the mighty furnace of the sun is glowing with the same heat as in July—a heat so intense that every square foot of its vast surface gives off enough energy to drive the colossal engine of the Centennial exhibition—a heat that, concentrated, would melt a column of ice fifty miles in diameter as fast as it shot towards the sun, even though it flew with the speed of light! The simple reason why we all shiver in February is that our globe lies at another angle towards the solar furnace, and only receives its indirect radiations. The change is in our position.

This astronomic fact gives a new freshness and vividness to that prayer of the Psalmist:

"Turn us, O God, and cause thy face to shine, and we shall be saved." God's love is inexhaustible and unchangeable. He is the same yesterday, to-day, and for ever. The reason why a Christian is cold, or why a church gets frozen up, is that they have swung off from God, and put themselves into the same position towards him that our globe has towards the winter sun. When a Christian backslides from duty, he throws himself out of the sunlight of God's countenance. His spiritual winter is of his own making. So with an ice-bound church, in which formality and fashion and frigidity have so lowered the spiritual temperature that the plants of grace are frostbitten. Sermons lie like icicles upon its floor; its prayer-room becomes a refrigerator, and no poor sinner is ever attracted in thither to be warmed and melted. This is hardly a caricature of those churches in which conversions have sunk down to zero.

The first duty of a cold Christian, or a church of cold Christians, is to recognize and confess a wrong position towards God. He that never

mourns never mends.   He who covereth his sins
must take the consequences.   But when we are
ready to say and do say, "O God! I have wan-
dered away from thee; I have fled from thy face
into the cold atmosphere of worldliness and selfishness and unbelief; help me to turn from my
backslidings;" when our hearts utter this prayer,
there is the first step taken towards recovery.
Such an honest, contrite confession as this, made
without any attempt at concealment or excuse,
would be the harbinger of a revival in scores of
churches to-day.   God never blesses one of his
children while in an attitude of disobedience.
The change needed is not a change of our cir-
cumstances, although we often make a scapegoat
of the word and talk about "our unfavorable cir-
cumstances."   The change demanded is one of
character and conduct.   The love of the world—
the silly ambition to walk in a vain show—and
that "big house-devil" of self-indulgence, have
drawn the soul away from Christ.   "He that is
nearest to me is nearest to the fire," is one of the
traditional utterances of our Lord, not reported

by the evangelists. Whether Christ ever uttered this or not, it is undeniable that he who is farthest from him is the most frozen and lifeless.

The first step, then, is a reconversion. The word "conversion" signifies a turning from sin to the Saviour. Reconversion is not regeneration, for the Bible never speaks of such a thing as being "born again" a great many times. Reconversion means simply the return of a backsliding Christian to God and to the path of forsaken duties. Peter was thus reconverted after his shameful fall in Pilate's judgment-hall. The very gist of the prayer, "Turn us, O God," is that the Holy Spirit will move us with mighty power, and so work in us that we shall return to the Lord and begin a new style of holy living. As Spurgeon pithily puts it, "All will come right when we are right." All will come right with me the moment that I get into the right position towards God. All will come right with the minister's sermons, and with the prayer-meetings and with the Sabbath-school; a new converting power will descend into the church just as soon as it swings back from the polar regions of sin into the light of God's countenance.

There is only one way by which nature turns winter into spring; it is by bringing the face of the earth into a new position towards the sun-rays. ¯ Then the snow-banks vanish, the seeds sprout, the grass peeps out, the buds open, and the sun reneweth the face of the year. Even so there is but one way to be delivered from a spiritual winter which blights our graces and kills all spiritual activity. It is by coming back to God so that his face may shine upon us. Then we shall walk in the broad, full light of his countenance without stumbling. Then our affections will thaw out, and, with some Christians, one of the first symptoms will be seen in the opened purse. Then tongues long frozen up will begin to be heard in the prayer-meeting. A new quickening power will descend and make the buried seeds of gospel truth to start up into the awakening and conversion of souls. God's face, God's favor will accomplish all this and divers other rich and wonderful blessings. In short, *we shall be saved.*

14

Christians will be saved from the guilt of neglected duty. We shall be saved from the deadly malaria of the world, and saved from the dominion of the adversary. The impenitent will be reached, and so turned from the error of their ways as to save their souls from death eternal. This, my dear brethren, is the urgent, imperative need of the hour—even a thorough, hearty turning back into the full blaze and light and heat of God's face. Oh, what a revival that will bring! Faithless praying and fruitless preaching will disappear like ice in April. God will cause his face to shine upon us and restore unto us the joys of his salvation. Then shall transgressors be taught his ways, and sinners (both in the church and out of it) be converted to the Lord. The winter will be past and gone, and the time of the singing of souls will come again.

ONE BY ONE.

——◆——

WHEN a lad I used to join in the apple-gatherings in the ripe month of October. The common fruit, which was destined to the cider-press or the swine, was shaken from the trees, and no amount of bruising did any harm. But the choice pippins and Spitzenbergs, which were destined for the apple-bins, were carefully picked by hand. Those were gathered one by one; we intended that they should *keep* through the winter.

This process illustrates the only effectual method for the conversion of souls. "Ye shall be gathered *one by one,*" was the declaration made to God's people in the olden time. The Lord declares that in the time of the purification and restoration of Israel he would gather in his grain seed by seed; each seed should be tested, and not a single one overlooked, or one genuine kernel be lost. This emphasizes the fact that in

God's sight there is no such thing as "the masses." God sees only *individuals;* every one unlike every other, and every one the possessor of an immortal soul. Guilt is an individual thing appertaining to a personal conscience; when a nation sins, or when a church goes astray, it simply means that there are a great many personal sinners. Nor are sinners saved by regiments. When three thousand were converted in a single day at Jerusalem, each one repented for himself, each one came into personal union with the risen Christ.

When engaged in earnest efforts for the conversion of souls, it is vitally important for Christians to study and imitate the example of Jesus and his apostles. A very large portion of Christ's inspired biography is occupied by his personal interviews—with a guilty woman by a well, with a publican by the wayside, with a young ruler, with a blind beggar, or with a Nicodemus in a private room. To the Son of God, as to every faithful gospel minister, *one soul was a great audience.* The single extended discourse

which Christ delivered was aimed at every audi-
tor before him.

No fact is more patent on the face of the
book of the Acts than that it is the record chiefly
of individual labors for the conversion or the
spiritual training of individuals. Those first
Christians were men and women who understood
thoroughly their personal responsibility and the
power of personal effort. Find, if you can, the
appointment of a single "committee" in the
book of the Acts. Seven men were indeed des-
ignated to the work of dispensing charities to
the poor; but this was done in order to release
the others for personal labor in declaring the
word of life. Very little is said about church
organizations. Nothing was allowed to keep
man from man—the individual believer from the
individual sinner. Peter goes right after Corne-
lius; Philip talks directly to Queen Candace's
treasurer; Aquila and Priscilla have a great
Bible-class in the person of eloquent Apollos;
and Dorcas is a sewing-society in herself. Amid
all the Conventions and "Union meetings" and

endless talk about revivals, is there not danger
that each Christian my forget that he or she is
the bearer of *one lamp?* And if that lamp be
well filled with grace, and its light be lovingly
thrown on one sinner's path, more good will be
accomplished than by a whole torchlight proces-
sion out on parade. A crowd is often in the
way when a soul is to be rescued. Christ led a
deaf man out of the crowd when he wished to
deal with him alone. Those early Christians
wrought wonders for God and dying humanity,
but they accomplished them by the simple direct
method—*every man to his man.* Personal holiness made each worker a partner with the Omnipotent Jesus.

As I recall my own ministerial experience, I
can testify that nearly all the converting work
done has been by personal contact with souls.
For example, I once recognized in the congregation a new-comer, and at my first visit to his
house was strongly drawn to him as a very noble-
hearted, manly character. A long talk with him
seemed to produce little impression; but before I

left he took me up stairs to see his three or four
rosy children in their cribs. As we stood looking at the sleeping cherubs, I said to him, "My
friend, what sort of a father are you going to be
to these children? Are you going to lead them
towards heaven, or—the other way?" That
arrow lodged. At our next communion season
he was at the Master's table, and he soon became
a most useful officer in the church. There is an
unbolted door in about everybody's heart, if we
will only ask God to show us where to find it.

Every pastor, and every successful Sunday-
school teacher will recall similar experiences of
personal interviews that did the business. Harlan Page never attempted any other method than
hand-picking. Even Mr. Moody has often told
me that his most effective work is done in the
inquiry-room, where he deals with souls *one by
one.* The true way to insure conversions in our
congregations is for individual Christians (*you*,
for instance) to give themselves afresh to Jesus,
and then go after some one soul that is within
the reach of their influence. Be on the watch

for opportunities. Do a personal kindness, or make a personal visit to open the way to the heart's door. Sometimes a kind, faithful letter is blessed to a soul's awakening. A single sentence, kindly spoken to him in the street, brought one of my neighbors to the Saviour. Heaven has its myriads of saved sinners; but they were gathered there one by one.

Let me also remind those Christians who desire to make this opening year a time for growth in godliness, that they may commit the serious mistake of trying to grow "by wholesale." A vague desire to be better, stronger, holier, will come to nothing. Character is built, like the walls of an edifice, by laying one stone upon another. Lay hold of some single fault and mend it. Put the knife with God's help to some ugly besetting sin. Stop that one leak that has let so much foul bilge-water into your soul. Put into practice some long-neglected duty. The first step to improvement with one person was to banish his decanters; with another, to discontinue his secular paper on Sunday morning; with another, to ask the pardon of an injured friend; with another, to go after some street Arabs and take them to a mission-school. He can never be rich towards God who despises a pennyworth of true piety. Holiness is just living aright in the least things as well as the greatest; for graces can only be gathered *one by one.*

" I count this thing to be grandly true,
    That a righteous deed is a step towards God,
    Lifting the soul from its common clod
To a purer air and a clearer view.

" Heaven is not reached by a single bound,
    But we build the ladder by which we rise
    From the lowly earth to the vaulted skies,
And we mount to its summit *round by round.*"

GLEANING FOR CHRIST.

RUTH, the Moabitess, was in many respects a
model for our American maidens. Too industri-
ous to be ashamed of honest work—too indepen-
dent to rely on her poor mother for her daily
bread—she goes out to the barley-field to glean
after the reapers. She knows that it is the cus-
tom of the country to leave some stalks of corn
for the poor to gather. Boaz also commands his
harvesters to "let fall some of the handfuls on
purpose for her." The wisest of all charities is
that which helps the poor to help themselves.
Ruth has a brave heart and nimble fingers, does
not mind a backache or a scratch of her fingers
among the brambles; and at sunset she comes
home to her mother with an ephah of barley.
Proud mother is Naomi as she inquires of the
busy-fingered girl, "Where hast thou gleaned to-
day?"

This is a fitting question for every Christian on a Sabbath evening. Equally fit is it for every Sunday-school teacher at the close of his or her day's work. All genuine Bible-study is gleaning. Some of the most nutritious and soul-strengthening truths are unexpected discoveries. We come upon them just where we did not expect to find them. Right in the midst of a catalogue of names in the fourth chapter of Chronicles we light upon the word "Jabez," the child who was born in sorrow, but proved to be a sunshine and a blessing. That little stroke of Bible history has been a mine of spiritual instruction to many a child of God. There is good gleaning too, in the book of Leviticus—which some careless people set down as a mere catalogue of Jewish upholsteries. Such Bible explorers as Bonar and Arnot and Bushnell and Moody will bring you an "ephah of barley" out of the neglected corners of God's wonderful grain-field. He lets fall many a handful for the benefit of those who believe that every line in their Bibles is inspired, and was written for a purpose. The ministers

who never wear out are the men who are never
afraid of a backache in searching for a fresh
truth.

Genuine work for the ingathering of souls is
like Ruth's work in her kinsman's barley-field.
It may be described by four P's. In the first place
it is patient. No pastor or Sunday-school teacher is fit for his post unless he has rubbed the word
"can't" out of his vocabulary. The hardest
part of all Christian work is to toil a great while
with little or no result. Captain Buford at West
Point broke off the trunnion of a cannon by re-
peated blows of a hammer. If there had been
one stroke the less, the iron would not have
yielded. It takes a long hammering to break
some hearts, and to beat some vital truths into
some dull consciences. Unless Ruth had been
content to pick up one spear at a time she never
would have got her bag of barley.

2. The next qualification for a good gleaner
is to be painstaking. Ralph Wells will find a
hundred kernels of golden grain in a passage
which a careless reader will pronounce as empty

as the east wind. He will spare no pains either to win some young street Arab who was regarded as a fair candidate for the police station. Christ Jesus took a long journey into the coast of Tyre and Sidon, just to bring a blessing to one poor woman. What pains he took with that bigoted and loose-principled woman of Sychar, until he had probed her heart to the core. The longest of all his recorded conversations was with a person whom his disciples would disdain to notice. If Christians would exercise their ingenuity and set themselves resolutely to work, as Harlan Page did, for the conversion of individual souls, our churches might be doubled every year.

3. All good work comes to nothing which is given up when half done. If Harlan Page had stopped that winter evening talk with young E. H—— at the corner of the street before his young friend surrendered to Christ, then that soul might have lost the precious gift of eternal life, and New York lost one of its best pastors. "Why do you tell that boy the same thing twenty times?" "Because," replied Susannah Wesley,

"the other nineteen times will go for nothing unless the twentieth time makes the impression." God's Spirit is wonderfully persevering in the conversion and discipline of souls. It required a long process to build up such a man as Paul. A great sculptor never begrudges the chisel strokes which fit his "Eves" and "Greek Slaves" to shine in the gallery of masterpieces. A Christian is carving for eternity.

4. But no patience, and no painstaking and persevering labor for Jesus will secure the result without the gift of the knees. Prayer brings God to our aid, and then the victory is sure. From Paul's day to this, the men and women who bring in the big sheaves have been "instant in prayer." Out of the hardest fields and the thorniest experiences a prayerful soul will gather the "ephah" for God's granaries. Brother! sister! have you attained to the four P's in your spiritual training? Then, at the close of life's toils, when you stand up for the final reckoning, you will not be afraid to meet the question, "What have you gleaned to-day?"

SEEKING AFTER HOLINESS.

THE word holiness is formed from *holy*, which signifies *whole, sound, entire.* Holiness is equivalent to the old Saxon word *wholth* or health; therefore a holy person is one who has been healed, and is in a sound spiritual condition. The real disease that afflicts and maims and torments and kills is sin. Holiness is the recovery from the controlling and deadly power of this disease. But as we never yet saw any one so perfectly healthy as never to feel an ache or a pain, so we need not expect here to be beyond the smart of inward sinfulness of desire— the pain of much conscious wrong-doing, and the mortifying sense of incompleteness and shortcoming. The very expression which Paul employs, "ye are complete in Him," means, "ye are made full in Him." It refers to complete-

ness of *provision* in Christ, and not to any completeness of performance or character in us.

Shall we seek after holiness? Is there any
encouragement to do this? Yes; not only encouragement as strong as the love of Jesus can
make it, but obligation also.

A holy Christian is one who is in good
health. The heart has been delivered from the
supreme control of the devil, and brought under
the blessed dominion of Christ. The conscience
is quick to detect sin—even under some smooth
disguises—and rises into protest and strong strug-
glings against it. The affections go out towards
Jesus; there is a sweet delight in his service,
and an honest endeavor to keep his commandments. A Christian's liberty is the possibility
of serving God; the bond-slave of sin has not
reached that, and never can until Christ strikes
off his fetters. One of the best evidences of
holiness we know of is the aim to obey Christ,
and the sharp sense of contrition and self-abase-
ment when he has been disobeyed. He who
mourns not, mends not. We don't believe that

the godliest man or woman lives who does not often have need to smite on the breast, and cry out, "God be merciful to me a sinner!"

For the holiness that fights against sin, battles with temptation, keeps unspotted from the world, and lays self on the altar, there is a crying need in our time. It is a sympathetic spirit, going about doing good, yet it has no sympathy with evil customs and the fashions of the world. It strives to keep clean. Against the downward pull of the world it braces itself and says, "If others do this, yet will not I." It dares to be singular and unfashionable. It keeps out of places where it would be smirched; and finds such enjoyment in its prayer-service, its Bible-study, its deeds of charity, and in the innocent joys of life, that it does not hanker after the playhouse and kindred sensualities. Walking in the Spirit, it does not stoop to the lusts of the flesh.

This soul-health is not got by single occasional acts, such as going to a "Bible-reading," or a meeting for promoting holiness, or by com-

ing to the communion-table. Whatever benefit
may be got by these or other exercises, the case
demands something deeper than externals. The
soul must take in Christ, and let him abide
there. The will must submit to him, and let
him control, and the life must feel his invigor-
ating power as my body feels the nourishing
effect of wholesome bread and the restoring
effects of honest sleep. The pulse of the heart
must beat for Christ steadily—not with fever-
ish rapidity to-day and feeble languor to-morrow.

Surely we may aspire after such health of
heart and wholesome and happy living as are
briefly outlined above. The more we possess it
the less shall we boast of it. Other people will
detect it, as we do the presence of the fire that
is burning in the stove. The inward heat comes
out and affects every particle of air in the room.
We can no more conceive of genuine holiness
that is unfelt by others than we can of a burning
fire that emits no warmth.

GLIMPSES OF HEAVEN.

ONE of the many internal evidences that the Bible is of divine origin is furnished by its method of dealing with heaven. If it were a human composition, it would devote a large space to that existence in which immortal beings are to spend everlasting ages; it would dwell on numberless particulars in its description of the "better country." But God's Book devotes over one hundred average pages to the rules of life in this world—even though this life on earth is measured by two or three score of years. Its aim is to show us the *way* to heaven; and when we get there it will be time enough to find out what manner of place it is, and what will be the precise employments of its occupants. A very few sentences only in God's Word are devoted to the description of the saints' everlasting home. The Bible says just enough to pique our curiosity and to stimulate speculation, but not enough to lift the sublime mystery which o'erhangs it like a cloud of glory. A few things seem clear to us. It is a *place*—a distinctly bounded one—or else such words as "walls" and "gates" are a mere phantasy. The light of it proceeds from a central throne; for the Lamb who is in the midst of the throne is the light thereof.

There is something beautifully suggestive in the many-sidedness of heaven, with gates of entrance from every point of the compass. This emphasizes the catholicity of God's "many mansions," into which all the redeemed shall enter, from all parts of the globe, and from every denomination in Christ's flock. All shall come in through Christ, yet by many gateways. The variety of "fruits" on the trees of life points towards the idea of satisfying every conceivable taste and aspiration of God's vast household.

Heaven is assuredly to be a home; its occupants one large, loving household. It will meet our deepest social longings; no one will complain of want of "good society." The venerable Em-

mons is not the only profound thinker who has fed
his hopes of "a good talk with the apostle Paul."
Dr. Guthrie is not the only parent who has felt
assured that his "wee Johnnie" would meet
him inside the gate. Many a pastor counts on
finding his spiritual children there as a crown of
rejoicing in that day. The recognition of friends
in heaven cannot be a matter of doubt. Nor
will any hateful spirit of caste mar the equalities
of a home where all have a common Lord and
and all are brethren.

When Cyneas, the ambassador of Pyrrhus,
returned from his visit to Rome in the days of
her glory, he reported to his sovereign that he
had seen a "commonwealth of kings." So will
it be in heaven, where every heir of redeeming
grace will be as a king and priest unto God, and
divine adoption shall make every one a member
of the Royal family. What a comfort that we
need never to pull up our tent-poles in quest of a
pleasanter residence. Heaven will have no
"moving-day." When you and I, brother,
have packed up at the tap of death's signal-bell,

we set out on our last journey, and there will be a delightful permanence in those words "*for ever with the Lord.*" The leagues to that home are few and short. Happy is that child of Jesus whose life-work is kept up so steadily to the line that he is ready to leave it at an instant's notice; happy is he who is ever listening for the invitation to hasten to his home.

One of the best evidences of the changed and entirely sanctified condition of Christians in that new world of glory will be that God can *trust us* there with complete, unalloyed prosperity! I never saw a Christian yet in this world who could be; even Paul himself needed a "thorn" to prick his natural pride and keep him humble. There is not one of us whose religion might not soon decay, like certain fruits, if exposed to the blazing heat of a perpetual sunshine. Here we require constant chastisements, constant lettings-down, and frequent days of cloud and storm. God could not more effectually ruin us than by letting us have our own way.

But in heaven we can *bear* to be perpetually

prosperous, perpetually healthy, perpetually happy, and freed from even the need of self-watch-
fulness! The hardest recognition of heaven will
be to *know ourselves*. We shall require no rods
of discipline there, and there will be no house-
room for crosses in the realms of perfect holiness.
Can it be that you and I shall ever see a day that
shall never know a pang, never witness a false
step, never hear a sigh of shame or mortifica-
tion, never see one dark hour, and never have a
cloud float through its bright, unbroken azure of
glory? Can all this be? *Yes*, this may all and
will all be true of me, if I am Christ's faithful
child; but oh! what a *changed creature* must I be
when I get on the other side of that gate of
pearl! Heaven will not be a greater surprise to
us than we shall be to ourselves.

THE WRECK OF THE GOLD-SHIPS.

———◆———

THERE are many passages in the Word of God that most readers pass by, as they would pass unlighted transparencies in the street at night. If somebody sets a lamp or kindles a gas-jet behind the transparency, its picture or inscription becomes luminous, attracting all eyes to it. One purpose of good preaching is to set lamps behind neglected passages.

Among the overlooked episodes in Old Testament history which are full of suggestive wisdom is one in the life of that good and great Judæan monarch, Jehoshaphat. His reign exalted the southern kingdom to a high prosperity. He wrought a good educational work among his people, and established a commission for expounding the Mosaic laws. He did many other noble things; but upon the lustre of his character and reign fell one great and grievous shad-

ow. It was the sin of *alliance with wicked men.*
Jehoshaphat had riches and honor in abundance,
and his heart was lifted up in the ways of the
Lord; yet he "joined affinity with Ahab," the
profligate tyrant of the northern kingdom. He
gave his son in marriage to Ahab's daughter,
and made a military alliance with Ahab, which
ended in the battle of Ramoth-Gilead, in which
the northern king played a treacherous part and
lost his life. Not satisfied with these entangling
alliances, which were both prompted by selfish
policies, he entered into a commercial partnership with Ahab's successor, the godless Ahaziah.
Jehu, a prophet of Jehovah, had the courage to
administer the sharp rebuke, "Shouldst thou
help the ungodly, and love them that hate the
Lord? Therefore is wrath upon thee from before the Lord."

The narrative of Jehoshaphat's venture with
wicked Ahaziah reads very much like some of
the "big bonanza" schemes of these days in
Colorado and Nevada. The two monarchs join
hands in a gold-hunting expedition. The sacred

chronicler tells us that they built ships in partnership, on the Gulf of Akabah, for the purpose of seeking gold in Ophir.   But the ill-starred
enterprise was blasted by the Lord; the "ships
went not; for they were wrecked at Ezion-
geber."   This was no accidental catastrophe;
for the fearless Eliezer told Jehoshaphat plainly,
"Because thou hast joined thyself with Ahaziah
the Lord hath broken (or wrecked) thy works."
Upon that illuminated transparency which pic-
tures the wreck of the gold-ships there blazes
out this truth : *partnership with sin is a fatal mistake.*

We could fill the pages of this book with
illustrations of this truth drawn from our own
observation.   Many a sorrowing father can tell
the story of what befell his beloved·boy.   The
youth, fascinated with a set of gay fellows, who
were "posted" in all the amusements of the
town, fell into their snares, and spent his even-
ings with them in their favorite haunts.   His
night-key admits him to the door of home in the
"small hours," while his foolish parents are on

their pillows.   It is the old, old story, short but
crushing.   Like Eli, the father "restrains not"
the son when he is "making himself vile," and
like Eli, he pays the bitter penalty.   When the
ruin has been wrought by a round of wine-sup-
pers, theatres, and brothels, the parents get their
eyes open to see that evil company has wrecked
their gold-ship.   The streets of all our cities,
like the rocks of Ezion-geber, are strewed with
the ruins of high hopes that went to pieces in
wicked associations.   When parents intrust a
night-key to a son who has no self-restraint or
Bible-conscience, they give him a free pass on
the road to perdition.

There is another phase of domestic life in
which this Old Testament episode finds its frequent parallels.   We recall now an only daughter
of rare beauty and accomplishments.   Her perilous charms attracted a suitor who was coarse and
sensual; but he was heir to an expected fortune.
His anticipated wealth bribed the foolish parents
and overcame the daughter's scruples.   She
consented, contrary to her own judgment, to

marry him. Within a few years he was disgraced, and she was divorced. God's law is, "Whatsoever ye sow, that shall ye also reap." It was that law, more irresistible than the winds of heaven, that wrecked the poor girl's gold-ship in broken hopes and a broken heart. Of all the alliances with sin from mercenary motives, the most certainly fatal are those which are made under the sacred name of wedlock.

The political history of our country is sadly eloquent with examples of civilians and statesmen who have wrecked their careers by alliances with wrong men, wrong policies, or wrong institutions. Every man, on his entrance upon public life, has his "mount of temptation." If he courageously says, "Get thee behind me, Satan!" his subsequent path to honor and true success is assured. If he yields, he is lost. The sorceress, during more than one generation, was *slavery*. By her much fair speech and promises of promotion she caused many an ambitious statesman to yield to her, and "straightway he went after her as an ox goeth to the slaughter."

This truth of perilous partnerships is full of warnings to business men. Especially is it admonitory to young men who are anxious to reach wealth by short cuts and are not scrupulous as to the methods. The market is crowded with sharp schemers, the papers abound with glowing announcements of commercial ventures and "gilt-edged" enterprises. The number of credulous Jehoshaphats who are enticed into gold expeditions to Ophir, with Ahaziahs in the partnership, is almost past belief. The wrecks are well nigh as numerous. It is not only from wild schemes of speculation that danger arises. Many a merchant, banker, manufacturer, or tradesman has been induced by friends or partners to ally himself with methods and practices which his own conscience, in his better moments, did not approve; but he hushed conscience with the promise of big profits, or with the current sophistry, "Oh! everybody does such things!" The men who, like William E. Dodge, refuse to "break God's laws for a dividend" are not to be found in regiments. Commerce and trade, like politics, contain a thousand repetitions of that old Scripture line, "Because thou hast joined thyself with Ahaziah, the Lord hath wrecked thy works."

"Be ye not partakers of other men's sins" is a divine admonition that has not lost its solemn portent. Though hand join in hand, wrong-doing will not go unpunished; if not punished in this world, then surely it will be in the next. Just as certainly as that the wages of sin is death, so certain is it that eternity will reveal the fearful wreck of innumerable gold-ships—the "loss total, and no insurance."

THE HONEY OF THE WORD.

"SEE, how mine eyes have been enlightened, because I tasted a little of this honey." So spake Jonathan, the true-hearted son of a false-hearted father. Saul had pronounced a curse upon any of his army who should taste of food during their pursuit of the enemy. But when the troops reached a forest where the bees had laid up their abundant stores, several honeycombs were found lying upon the earth. The prince-royal, not having heard of his father's harsh edict, put forth the rod which was in his hand, and dipped it in a honeycomb and put it to his mouth; and *his eyes were enlightened*. Refreshment came to his hungry frame, and enlightenment to his eyes which were dim with faintness and fatigue.

What a beautiful parable this incident is to set forth one of the richest blessings of the Word of Life! The Psalmist extolled it as "sweeter than honey;" but he also exclaimed, "The entrance of Thy Word giveth light; yea, understanding to the simple." It is not the mere reading of the Word carelessly, or the hearing of it listlessly, but its entrance into the soul, which produces this inward illumination. Thousands of people listen to God's truths every Sabbath without any effect on the heart or the life. They do not take the truth into their souls, as Jonathan took the honey into his system. But when the Word is partaken of, and the Spirit accompanies it, there is a revelation made to the heart like that which the poor blind boy had after the operation of a skilful oculist. His mother led him out of doors, and taking off the bandage, gave him his first view of sunshine and flowers. "O mother!" he cried, "why did you not tell me it was so beautiful?" The tears started as she replied, "I tried to tell you, my dear, but you could not understand me." So the spiritual sight must be opened, in order that the spiritual glories may be discerned. Many a poor sinner has

never found out what a glorious gospel our gospel
is until he has swallowed the honey for himself.
Even as a mental discipline there is no book
like God's Book. No other study so strength-
ens the understanding, clarifies the perceptions,
and enlarges the views, so purifies the taste, in-
vigorates the judgment, and educates the whole
man. The humblest day-laborer who saturates
his mind with this school-book from heaven becomes a superior man to his comrades — not
merely a purer man, but a clearer-headed man.
It was this honey from heaven which gave to the
Puritans much of their sagacity, as well as all of
their stubborn loyalty to the right. The secret
of the superiority of the Scottish peasantry is
found in that "big ha' Bible" which is the daily
study at every cottage ingleside. What an argument this is for keeping God's own school-book
for his children in every school of our land, high
or humble. As the honey strewed the forest for
Israel's common soldiers to partake of, so the
Lord has sent down his Word for the masses.
It is more than light, for it is an *enlightener*.
18

Not only does it reveal the grandest and most elevating truths in the universe, but it improves the actual vision. It makes the blind to see, and the strong-sighted stronger. Who of us that has been terribly perplexed about questions of right and wrong, and been sorely puzzled as to our duty, has not caught a new view and a true view as soon as he dipped his rod into the honeycomb of God's Word? A single text once settled for me a vexed question of duty. Cowper found in the twenty-fifth verse of the third chapter of Romans the honey which brought light to his soul when overclouded with despair. John Wesley thrust his rod into this verse: "The law of the spirit of life in Christ Jesus hath *made me free* from the law of sin and death." Even Paul had not learned his own sin until the commandment against covetousness opened his eyes. The fifty-third chapter of Isaiah so enlightened the eye of the Ethiopian treasurer that he discovered Jesus the Lamb of God !

Ah, there is many a reader of these pages who can testify how the precious honey from heaven brought light and joy to his eyes when dimmed with grief. The exceeding great and precious promises were not only sweet, they were illuminating. They lighted up the valley of the shadow of death. They showed how crosses can be turned into crowns, and how losses can brighten into glorious gains. When in a sick-room I always dip my rod into the honeycomb of the fourteenth chapter of John. It brings Jesus there. One of my bravest Sunday-school teachers so fed on this honey that on her dying-bed she said, "My path through the valley is long, but '*t is bright all the way.*"

Nothing opens the sinner's eyes to see himself and to see the Saviour of sinners like the simple Word. The Bible is the book to reveal iniquity in the secret parts. If the young man will dip his rod into this warning, "Look not on the wine when it is red," he may discover that there is a nest of adders in the glass ! If the scoffer can be induced to taste some of that honey which Christ gave to Nicodemus, he may find heaven and hell to be tremendous *realities!*

Brethren of the ministry, I do not know how you all may feel; but I am growing confident that our chief business is not only to eat hugely of this honey ourselves, but to tell our people where to dip their rods. We have got no new gospel for them—no "advanced thought" beyond Moses, John, and Paul. The honey lies thick on the ground. May the divine Spirit help us to point it out to blinded dying men!

CAN WE FEEL SURE?

\

IT was said of a certain magnificent speech of Daniel Webster that "every word weighed a pound." But there is a line in the thirty-fifth Psalm—mostly made up of monosyllables—in which every word weighs a ton. David uttered it in a season of despondency, when he cried out, "*Say unto my soul, I am thy salvation.*" The old monarch was in trouble. His own throne was assailed, and so he went to the Everlasting Throne. His own heart was assailed by doubts, and so he sought for a fresh and full assurance of salvation. Whatever David's own experiences may have been, he furnished a golden prayer for universal use in these pregnant, pithy words: "Say unto my soul, I am thy salvation."

The salvation which all of us most need is a deliverance from the guilt and dominion of sin—

to be liberated from the bondage of that great
slave-holder the devil. Beset with temptations,
we need succor when we are tempted. The only
salvation "under heaven given among men" is
by the atoning blood of Jesus and the regenerating power of the Holy Spirit. This is a full
salvation, a complete salvation; it is God's mas-
terpiece of mercy to us guilty, depraved, and
dying sinners. Can this salvation be made *sure*
to a man, and can he be *sure* that he possesses it?

We answer unhesitatingly, Yes. David did
not ask for impossibilities when he asked God to
assure him of his salvation. Paul knew what
he was about when he said, "Know ye not your
own selves, how that Jesus Christ is in you,
except ye be reprobates?" There is no perhaps
about the salvation of a true follower of Christ
any more than there is about the rising of to-
morrow's sun. It does not depend upon my say,
or your say, or any man's say. Only God can
give the decisive and infallible assurance to us
that we are safe for this world and for eternity.

Let it be carefully noted that the prayer is

that God would say unto the *soul*, "I am thy
salvation." There is no audible voice addressed
to the ear; in fact, multitudes hear the offer of
salvation every Sabbath by the ear, and yet their
hearts are as deaf as adders. What God says can
only be heard by the heart. We would define
faith to be *heart-hearing*. And unto the docile,
believing soul God says wonderful things, and
things to make the soul leap for joy. "This is
a faithful saying and worthy of all acceptation,
that Christ Jesus came into the world to save
sinners." I open the ivory chamber of John's
Gospel, and read these words: "Verily, verily, I
say unto you, he that heareth my word and
believeth on him that sent me hath everlasting
life and shall not come into condemnation."
Again, Jesus says in the same Gospel, "This is
the will of him that sent me, that every one which
seeth the Son and believeth on him may have
everlasting life." "My sheep hear my voice,
and I know them and they follow me. And I
give unto them eternal life, and they shall never
perish; neither shall any man pluck them out

of my hand." He does not affirm that we may
never, in a fit of waywardness and pride, throw
ourselves out of that almighty and loving hand.
But he does declare that while we stay there we
are safe. And, being safe, we have a right to
know it, and to feel all the serenity and satisfac-
tion which this ownership by the Lord Jesus
can inspire.

Faith is the soul's trust in Jesus as our salvation. It *ought* to bring a delightful sense of
security. But it does not always do so, because
it is too weak and doubting to produce assurance.
Faith is the milk, and assurance is the cream
which rises on it. The richer the milk the
more abundant will be the cream. Assurance is
not essential to salvation, as faith is; for God
will let a great many people into heaven who
had a very feeble faith here on earth. Faith is
life, though it be sometimes a very weak, anxious,
burdened, and uncomfortable life. Assurance
marks a higher degree of health, vigor, joy, and
power to overcome. Peter possessed some faith
when he screamed to his Master from the

waves, "Lord, save me!" He had reached a
much higher attainment by the Spirit when he
exclaimed in the market-place of Jerusalem,
"This is the stone which was set at naught of
you builders, which is become the head of the
corner." Saul of Tarsus had an infant faith
born in his soul when he was groping about in
the house of Ananias at Damascus. The infant
had grown into a giant when Paul had reached
up to the eighth chapter to the Romans, and could
shout, "I *know* whom I have believed, and am
persuaded that He is able to *keep* that which I
have committed to Him." Jesus had really
said to Paul, "I am thy salvation."

Paul had the witness of the Spirit that he
was Christ's. There was an inward conviction
and an outward life, and the two corresponded
with each other. They both corresponded also
to the Spirit's description of true piety in the
Bible. When a tree produces the leaves of a
pear and the fruit of the pear, we are sure that
it is a pear-tree. When a man feels the love
of Jesus in his soul and keeps the commandments

of Jesus in his life, he has the witness of the Holy Spirit that he is in Christ. Being in Christ, he is safe. There is no condemnation to such a man. The Lord has said unto such a consistent believer, "I am thy salvation." But when an oily-tongued dissembler, who cheats his creditors or lives a life of secret uncleanness, rises in a prayer-meeting and prates glibly about his holiness or his sanctified attainments, he simply unmasks his own hypocrisy.

We have just said that assurance is not a positive essential of faith; but yet it is the privilege and the duty of a genuine Christian to possess the assurance of Christ's love and protection. Old Latimer used to say that when he had this steadfast trust in his Master he could face a lion; when he lost it, he was ready to run into a mouse-hole. Why should the soul to whom Jesus has said, "I *am* thy salvation," be continually worrying itself sick with doubts and fears? If I have put my everlasting all in Christ's hands, he is responsible for the trust— as long as I leave it with him.

Two men go out to Colorado and purchase tracts of mining-land. One of them spends half his time worrying about his deed, and in running to the clerk's office to see whether his title is good. While he is tormenting himself in this idiotic way, the other man has worked his gold-mine so industriously that he has sent fifty loads of solid ore to the crushing-mill. Brethren, if we have taken Christ's word, and committed our souls to his keeping and our lives to his disposal, let us not worry about our title-deeds to heaven. Let us understand the power of the two pronouns "my" and "thy." It is *my* soul to which the Almighty Jesus says, "I am *thy* salvation." Go about your life-work, brother, and do it honestly and thoroughly. God is responsible for the results and the reward. If I check my baggage to Chicago, it is not mine until I get there. It belongs to the baggage-master. Surely, I ought to have as strong a faith that my immortal soul is safe in Christ's keeping as I have that my trunk is safe in the charge of a railway officer.

Assurance of salvation by the Son of God is no modern discovery. It is not a new invention "patented" by any school of Bible students. It is as old as the cross of Calvary. Paul built his Epistle to the Romans on this rock. The Psalmist of Israel was seeking after it, in his troubles, when he cried out to the living God, "Say unto my soul, I am thy salvation!"

ASLEEP IN JESUS.

No scriptural description of death is so suggestive and so consoling as that which is con-
veyed by the familiar word *sleep*. It recurs often.
Stephen the martyr breathes his sublime prayer,
and then "he fell asleep." Our Lord said to
his disciples, "Our friend Lazarus sleepeth; but
I go that I may awake him out of sleep." Paul,
in that transcendently sublime chapter on the
resurrection, treats death as but the transient
slumber of the body, to be followed by the glorious awakening at the sound of the last trumpet.
And then he crowns it with that voice of the
divine Spirit, that marvellous utterance which
has been said and sobbed and sung in so many
a house of bereavement: "I would not have you
to be ignorant concerning them which are asleep;
for if we believe that Jesus died and rose again,
even so them also which sleep in Jesus will God

bring with him.'' No three words are inscribed
on more tombs or on more hearts than these:
''Asleep in Jesus.''

These declarations of God's Word describe
death as simply the temporary suspension of bodily activities. Not a hint is given of a total end,
an extinction, or an annihilation. The material
body falls asleep, the immortal spirit being meanwhile in full activity; and the time is predicted
when the body, called up from the tomb, shall
reunite with the deathless spirit, and the man
shall live on through eternity. What we call
dying is only a momentary process. It is a
flitting of the immortal tenant from the frail tent
or tabernacle, which is so often racked with pain
and waxes old into decay. Paul calls it a depar-
ture: ''To depart and be with Christ.'' The
spiritual tenant shuts up the windows of the
earthly house ere he departs; he muffles the
knocker at the ear, so that no sound can enter;
he extinguishes the fire that glows about the
heart, stops the warm currents that flow through
the veins, and leaves the deserted house cold,

silent, and motionless. We, the survivors, bend over the deserted heart-house; but there is neither voice nor hearing. We kiss the brow, and it is marble. The beloved sleeper is sleeping a sleep that thunders or earthquake cannot disturb. But what is there in this slumber of the body that suggests any fear that the ethereal essence of the spirit has become extinct or even suspended its activities? When the mother lays her darling in its crib, she knows that sleep simply means rest, refreshment, and to-morrow morning's brighter eye, nimbler foot, and the carol of a lark in her nursery. When you or I drop off into the repose of the night, we understand that the avenues of the five bodily senses are closed for a few hours; but the mind is, meanwhile, as busy as when we wake.

Death means just this: no more and no less. As Maclaren has vigorously said, "Strip the man of the disturbances that come from a fevered body, and he will have a calmer soul. Strip him of the hindrances which come from a body that is like an opaque tower around his spirit, with only a narrow crevice here and a narrow door there—five poor senses with which he is connected with the outer universe—and, surely, the spirit will have wider avenues out to God. It will have larger powers of reception, because it has become rid of the closer confinements of the fleshly tabernacle. They who die in Jesus live a larger, fuller, nobler life, by the very cessation of care, change, strife, and struggle. Above all, they live a fuller, grander life, because they ' sleep *in Jesus*' and are gathered into his embrace, and wake with him, clothed with white robes, awaiting the adoption, to wit, the redemption of the body.'' In God's good time, the slumbering body shall be resuscitated and shall be fashioned like to Christ's glorious body— *i. e.*, it shall be transformed into a condition which shall meet the wants of a beatific soul in its celestial dwelling-place. Verily, with this transcendent blaze of revelation pouring into the believer's death-chamber and his tomb, we ought not to sorrow as they that have no hope.

In this view of death (which is God's own

view) how vivid becomes the apostle's exclama-
tion, "I am confident and willing rather to
be absent from the body and to be present with
the Lord." "Who is it that is to be absent? I,
Paul—the living Paul—I can be entirely quit from
that poor tabernacle of flesh and yet live! My
body is no more Paul than the corn-ship was when
it went to pieces on the shore of Melita and I
escaped safe to land." Paul was entirely willing
that the old scarred and weary body might be
put to sleep, so that *he* might go home and be
present with his Lord. Then mortality would
be swallowed up of life. Go to sleep, poor, old,
hard-worked body, the apostle seems to say, and
Jesus will wake thee up in good time, and thou
shalt be made like to the body of his glory,
according to the working whereby he subdues
all things unto himself.

Let us not be charged with pushing this
Scripture simile too far when we hint that it
illustrates the different feelings with which different persons regard the act of dying. When
we are *sleepy*, we covet the pillow and the couch.

20

When work is to be done, when the duties of the day are pressing on us, then we are not only broad awake, but the more awake the better. Sleep then is repulsive. Even so do we see aged servants of God, who have finished up their life-work, and many a suffering invalid racked with incurable pains, who honestly long to die. They are sleepy for the rest of the grave and the home beyond it. Yet desire for death is not natural to the young, the vigorous, or especially to the servants of God who are most intent upon their high calling. These recoil from death, however saintly or spiritual they may be, or however strong be their convictions that heaven is infinitely better than this world. It is not merely the natural shrinking from death (which the man Christ Jesus felt in common with us), but the supreme idea of serving their God to the utmost possible limit. *For* Christ here, *with* Christ yonder, is the highest instinct of the Christian heart. The noble missionary, Judson, phrased it happily when he said, "I am not tired of my work, neither am I tired of the world; yet, when

Christ calls me home, I shall go with the glad-
ness of a boy bounding away from school." He
wanted to toil for souls until he grew *sleepy*, and
then he wanted to lay his body down to rest and
to escape into glory.

A dying-bed is only the spot where the material frame falls asleep. Then we take up the
slumbering form and gently bear it to its narrow
bed in mother earth. Our very word "ceme-
tery" describes this thought. It is derived from
the Greek word κοιμητήριον (*koimeterion*), which signifies a sleeping-place. Greenwood is really a
vast dormitory in which tens of thousands are
laid to their last repose—some in their gorgeous
environments of rosewood and marble, and others
in the poor little trundle-beds of the paupers'
plot. It is a mingled and promiscuous sleeping-
place; but the Master "knoweth them that are
his." They who sleep in him shall awake to
be for ever with their Lord.

On this tremendous question of the resurrection of our loved ones and our reunion with them,
our yearning hearts are satisfied with nothing

less than *certainty*. Poetic fancies are gossamer:
analogies from the sprouting of seeds and bulbs,
probabilities, intuitions, and all philosophizings
are too shadowy to rear a solid faith on. We
demand absolute certainty, and there are just
two truths that can give it. The first one is the
actual fact of Christ's own resurrection from the
death-slumber; the second is his omnipotent assurance that all they who sleep in him shall be
raised up and be where he is for evermore.
Those early Christians were wise in their generation when they carved on the tomb of the mar-
tyrs "*In Jesu Christo obdormivit.*"—In Jesus
Christ he fell asleep.

> "Oh! precious tale of triumph this!
>   And martyr-blood shed to achieve it,
> Of suffering past—of present bliss.
>   '*In Jesu Christo obdormivit.*'
>
> "Of cherished dead be mine the trust,
>   Thrice-blessed solace to believe it,
> That I can utter o'er their dust,
>   '*In Jesu Christo obdormivit.*'

THE SEVEN "BLESSEDS."

THERE are seven benedictions in the book of Revelation which will repay every Christian's closest study The first occurs in the opening lines of John's Apocalypse: "Blessed is he that readeth, and they that hear the words of this prophecy, and *keep* those things which are written therein." Just at the close of the Apocalypse is another similar passage: "Blessed is he that *keepeth* the sayings of the prophecy of this book." These two verses are like the golden clasps, one on each lid, that hold together a dear old family Bible. The divine commendation is here pronounced on the Bible-reader and the Bible-keeper. God's Word always honors itself. No man is fit to preach it who ever whiffles over the truthfulness and authority of its every page.

The next benediction is pronounced upon the gospel-guests: "Blessed are they who are called unto the marriage-supper of the Lamb."

This is what our sound old fathers style "effectual calling." They who are drawn by the attraction of the cross, and yield to that drawing, are renewed by the Holy Spirit. Theirs is a place at the celestial banquet. Upon them is put the clean linen and white which is the right eousness of Christ. How careful should every disciple be to walk unspotted from the world, for every stain looks ugly upon a white ground. Why should we wait until our arrival in heaven to look clean!

There is a hint as to the method of keeping thus, clearly given in the third benediction: "Blessed is he that watcheth and keepeth his garments, lest he walk naked and they see his shame." No believer can preserve the purity of his character without prayerful vigilance. "Watch!" And one reason for this watchfulness is that Christ's coming is to be as unannounced as the midnight visit of a burglar. The thief never sends us word that he is coming to steal our clothes. It will be a terrible thing to lose our wedding-garment. Old Dr. Alexan-

der used to say with solemn tenderness, "I wont
answer for any Christian while in an awful state
of backsliding."

Upon the gospel-doers rests the sweet approval of the fourth benediction. It is the blessing upon those "that *do* His commandments."
The evidence and the joy of discipleship both lie
in obedience to Christ. This is what the world
has a right to demand from us—a religion of
fruits. Away with the wretched delusion that
"good works" have no place in the Christian's
salvation ! Faith without works is dead.

He, and he only, who is born of Christ will
be able to pass this searching ordeal. Christ's
approval at the last great day will be, "Ye *did*
it unto me."

The next blessing in John's wonderful Revelation is that angelic voice that floats over the
resting-place of the pious dead. "Blessed are
the dead which die in the Lord." To them
the perils of the voyage are over. They have
cast anchor in the haven. They are safe. Peter
shall never deny again, and Paul will no more

be obliged to battle with an unruly "body." Calvin and Wesley can clasp hands over the glorious fact that neither one of them shall ever fall from grace. That is a joyful anthem which sings itself so sweetly over a believer's dust, "Blessed is he, for he died in the Lord."

About the last one of the benedictions in this sublime book there has been no little controversy: "Blessed and holy is he that hath part in the first resurrection." Our Millenarian brethren make much of this passage; but none of their ingenious speculations seem to clarify the mystery that hangs over that word "first." It is enough for me that if I fall to sleep in Jesus, I shall awake with him. Little does the date trouble me, or the question of precedence. There is not an unmarked grave in all Christ's household of the slumberers. He will call them up at the last day. "Them which sleep in Jesus will God bring together with him." And when we all reach that celestial home, we shall see these seven "blesseds" shining like the seven candlesticks before the throne.